Above the Herd . . .

Siringo fired and ducked back behind the steers, but the animals were just seconds away from stampeding because of the shots.

Clint fired twice, quickly dispatching two men from the action, then took cover himself.

Both men fired into the group of outlaws, who were scattering, trying to make a smaller target of themselves. The steers started to run, but that was of no concern to Siringo and Clint as long as they weren't trampled. And, in fact, the herd began to run *toward* the outlaws, who then really had to scramble to keep from being trampled beneath them.

Clint and Siringo managed to avoid that fate themselves, but the stampeding herd kicked up a lot of dust, which impeded their view. They both hoped their tracker, Tom Horn, had a clearer view from above . . .

But he did not . . .

THE GUNSMITH

378

THE PINKERTON JOB

J. R. ROBERTS

JOVE BOOKS, NEW YORK

W
PB
ROBER

BC
711

THE BERKLEY PUBLISHING GROUP
Published by the Penguin Group
Penguin Group (USA) Inc.
375 Hudson Street, New York, New York 10014, USA

USA | Canada | UK | Ireland | Australia | New Zealand | India | South Africa | China

Penguin Books Ltd., Registered Offices: 80 Strand, London WC2R 0RL, England
For more information about the Penguin Group, visit penguin.com.

THE PINKERTON JOB

A Jove Book / published by arrangement with the author

Jove Books are published by The Berkley Publishing Group.
JOVE® is a registered trademark of Penguin Group (USA) Inc.
The "J" design is a trademark of Penguin Group (USA) Inc.

For information, address: The Berkley Publishing Group,
a division of Penguin Group (USA) Inc.,
375 Hudson Street, New York, New York 10014.

ISBN: 978-0-515-15319-4

PUBLISHING HISTORY
Jove mass-market edition / June 2013

PRINTED IN THE UNITED STATES OF AMERICA

10 9 8 7 6 5 4 3 2 1

Cover illustration by Sergio Giovine.

ALWAYS LEARNING   **PEARSON**

ONE

Charlie Siringo waited while the other man studied the ground. Siringo had been a cowboy for a long time, was a published writer, and was working as a detective. He was not a tracker. For that he had sought out another man, and he left it up to him to do the tracking.

But that didn't mean he didn't get impatient.

"Well?" he demanded. "What do you see?"

The other man looked up at him and said calmly, "I see more than you see, or you'd be down here doin' this."

The New Mexican ground was so hard here, he didn't see how anyone could pick up tracks on it. But if anyone could, it was Tom Horn.

Horn remained on one knee for a few moments longer, then stood up, brushed his hands together, and looked off into the distance.

"We're still on the right track," he said.

He walked back to where Siringo sat his own horse and held the reins of Horn's. Siringo handed the reins to the younger man, who swung up into his saddle.

"Are you sure?" he asked.

"I'm positive," Horn said. "Charlie, you came to me, remember? Why you always gotta question me?"

"It's my nature, Tom," Siringo said. "I'm a detective."

"So you're sure these guys we're trailin' are the right ones?"

"I'm sure the Sandusky gang are the ones I'm after, yeah," Siringo said. "I'm not sure we're on their trail. I only know you say we're on *somebody's* trail."

"I picked up this trail from where you took me," Horn said. "You said the Sanduskys were there. If *you're* right, then *I'm* right. It all depends on you, Charlie."

"Yeah, well . . ."

"Are we goin'?" Horn asked.

"Yeah, yeah," Siringo said, "we're goin'. Lead on."

Horn didn't actually take the lead. Rather, they rode off together, with Horn determining the direction they took.

Charlie Siringo was a Pinkerton operative who had been assigned to find out who was rustling cattle in Santa Fe County, New Mexico. Once he had determined that it was Harlan Sandusky and his gang, he recruited Tom Horn to track the gang for him.

Since joining the Pinkertons two years earlier—using Pat Garrett's name as a reference—Siringo had worked mostly on labor disputes, but the Stock Grower's Association of New Mexico had paid the Pinkertons a lot of money to stop the rustling, so they had decided to send their best man. Also, they figured Siringo's experience as a cowboy— which he had set down in print in the published book, *A Texas Cowboy; Or Fifteen Years on the Hurricane Deck of a Spanish Pony*—would be a benefit.

Siringo knew that Tom Horn, several years younger than

himself, would be the man to actually track the gang down. He also trusted Horn to back his play. He intended to try to get the Pinkertons to hire Horn once they were done with this job. Siringo knew that Horn—a soldier, scout, and tracker—had all the makings of an excellent Pinkerton detective.

Despite all that, Siringo was becoming impatient to catch up to the Sandusky gang. It was time to put this job to bed and get back to Chicago. If he had wanted to spend this much time on horseback, he would have remained a cowboy.

Tom Horn respected Charlie Siringo.

He'd never tell him that, of course. Although he respected the detective, he also had enough ego to believe he was every bit as good as Siringo was. However, when it came to tracking, there was no doubt he was superior.

Horn was not yet thirty, and had established a reputation as a scout and tracker. He and Siringo had crossed paths several times and, while not friends, got along. In truth, Tom Horn had few friends. He was a man who enjoyed his solitude. That was why he enjoyed the time he had to spend on the trail when working.

But Siringo was paying him well this time, so they traveled together.

They stopped and camped for the night, and over beans and bacon Horn said, "I think we should catch up to them tomorrow."

"I'm lookin' forward to it," Siringo said.

"Can't wait to go back to Chicago?"

"It's so different, Tom," Siringo said, "after all the years I spent on a horse, punchin' cows."

"Yeah, well," Horn said, "I ain't done with my time on horseback."

"As long as you still enjoy it," Siringo said, "why change?"

Horn raised his coffee cup in agreement.

"I'll take first watch," Horn said.

While they were the pursuers, that didn't mean the pursued wouldn't double back at some point, and they didn't want to be caught unawares. So they had been setting a watch each night.

"Fine," Siringo said, "wake me in four hours."

"You can have longer if you want," Horn said. "I really don't sleep that much."

"Naw," Siringo said, "four hours is fine."

"Okay."

Siringo rolled himself up in his bedroll and said, "And try to leave me some coffee this time."

"I'll make sure there's a fresh pot," Horn said, pouring himself some more and nibbling on the last of the bacon.

TWO

A day earlier, Clint Adams awoke and drank the last of his coffee and ate the last of his beans for breakfast. He broke camp and killed the fire. He'd stop in the next town and restock.

Looking around, he figured the next town would be Las Vegas. He could have gone east, to Albuquerque, but he'd already bypassed it, not wanting to spend time in a big town. Las Vegas would suit his purposes.

He rode into Las Vegas before noon, found the street of the small town busy with foot traffic, as well as some buckboards. He'd been there before, but not for a while. It had grown, and the mercantile now occupied a store twice the size as last time he was there.

There were a number of horses already tied off in front of the place. He found a space for Eclipse, looped the reins loosely over the hitching post, and went inside.

The inside of the store was busy, so he took some time to walk around and examine the wares. There were racks of clothing, mostly for women, many dresses and hats, but there were some jeans and shirts for men folded on some tables. Plenty of tools—pitchforks, shovels, pickaxes—lined one wall, while another wall accommodated rifles and handguns, as well as ammunition. The store was extremely well stocked, which was probably attracting a lot of out-of-town—and even out-of-the-county—business.

Finally there was a lull and he stepped up to the front counter.

"How can I help you, sir?" the clerk asked happily. Of course he was happy—he was selling stuff hand over fist.

"I just need some coffee and beans," Clint said.

"Is that all? We have a wide variety of items, as you can see."

"I did see," Clint said, "but all I need is some coffee and beans."

"All right, sir," the clerk said. "How many cans of beans?"

"Four."

"Comin' up!"

He turned to the wall stocked with staples and took down a tin of coffee and four cans of beans. He put the items down in front of Clint.

"And I'll take some beef jerky," he said. Adding jerky to the beans would stretch them a bit.

"Yes, sir!"

The clerk told Clint how much and he paid the bill.

"Put that in a burlap sack, will you?" Clint asked.

"Of course, sir."

Clint left the store with his burlap sack, tied it to his saddle horn, and then mounted up. His intention was to ride out of town immediately, but he spotted the saloon across the street and suddenly his mouth had a dryness to it that water just wouldn't cut.

He needed a cold beer.

* * *

Once again he looped Eclipse's reins loosely around a pole before entering the saloon. The place was large, with lots of space between the tables, a full stage in front. Gaming tables were covered and would be until later that evening. At the moment, there were only a few patrons in the place, and Clint strode to the bar, where a bartender was waiting for him.

"Beer," Clint said.

"Comin' up."

When the beer came, it had a nice head, and was sweating. Clint sipped it and found it bitingly cold. It ate dust all the way down to his belly.

"That's good."

"Anything else?" the bartender asked.

"Nope, this'll be it."

"A nickel."

Clint tossed the nickel on the bar and said, "Good price."

The bartender took the nickel and moved down the bar.

Clint drank the beer slow enough to enjoy it, but fast enough so that the last sip was still cold.

He had just set the empty mug down on the bar when a man came running through the batwing doors.

"Hey," he yelled breathlessly, "they just brung 'em in."

"Brung who in?" the bartender asked. "Yer not makin' any sense, Wilson."

Wilson tried to catch his breath, then he said, "They just brung in Charlie Siringo and Tom Horn, all shot up!"

"Where are they?" Clint asked immediately.

"Took 'em over to Doc's."

Clint left the bar, grabbed Wilson by the shirt, and said, "Show me!"

THREE

There was a shingle hanging outside the building that said: DR. JOHN T. EDSON. Clint noticed it in passing as he followed Wilson inside.

The first person he saw was Charlie Siringo, sitting in a chair, holding a bloody bandage to his left arm. Tom Horn was nowhere to be seen.

"Charlie!" he said.

Siringo was startled when he saw Clint.

"Clint. What the hell are you doin' here?"

"I was in the saloon when I heard this fella say they brought you and Tom Horn in, all shot up. Are you all right?"

"I got nicked on the arm," Siringo said. "I'm fine. The doc is workin' on Tom. He took two bullets."

"Bad?"

"Bad enough," Siringo said, "but I don't think either one's gonna be fatal. I was able to stop the bleedin' out there, until we could get picked up."

"What happened?"

"I think I'm gonna have to tell the sheriff that," Siringo said, "so if you don't mind, I'll just wait 'til he shows up and tell it once."

"That's fine," Clint said. "Let me see that."

Siringo removed the bandage and Clint took a look at the wound. He'd seen hundreds of bullet wounds over the year, and this was nowhere near the worst.

"You're good," he said as Siringo covered it up again.

"What are you doin' in Las Vegas?" Siringo asked.

"I'm passing through, Charlie," Clint said. "I assume you're working."

"Sure am."

"And Horn?"

"Workin' with me."

"How's that going?"

"It *was* goin' fine, until this."

The doctor came out at that moment, wiping his hands on a towel. He was a youngish man, maybe forty, with black hair and handsome features.

"Doc," Siringo said, "how's he doin'?"

"He'll be okay," the man said. "He took one high on the shoulder. That's not a problem. The bad one is in the thigh. The bullet went through, tore a bit chunk out of the back of his thigh, but you did a good job controlling the bleeding. I closed the wound and bound it. He should be okay, as long as it doesn't get infected."

"Can he ride?"

"Not unless he wants to tear that wound open," Dr. Edson said. "I don't want him on a horse for at least a week. Now let me take a look at you."

Again, Siringo uncovered the wound. The doctor cleaned it and dressed it and pronounced Siringo fit.

"I was expectin' the sheriff to show up," Siringo said.

"If you want to talk to our sheriff, I think you'll have to go to him," Edson said.

"What kind of man is he?" Clint asked.

"He doesn't do any more than he has to do," Edson said. "Let's leave it at that."

"All right, then," Siringo said. "I'll go and see him. But can I talk to Tom first?"

"Sure, go on in."

"Clint?"

"Sure, I'll come along."

Siringo led the way, and he and Clint went into the examination room.

Tom Horn was lying on his right side on a table as they entered, favoring his heavily bandaged left thigh.

"Looks like you saved my leg, Siringo," he said, "and maybe my life."

"You're welcome, if that's a thank-you," Siringo said.

"Is that Clint Adams with you?"

"Hello, Tom. Glad you're not dead."

"Yeah, me, too," Horn said. "What the hell are you doin' here?"

"I was passing through and heard the news," Clint said. "Thought I'd come and check up on the two of you."

"I'm fine," Horn said. "All I need is a new pair of britches and we can get back on the trail."

"Not so fast, Horn," Siringo said. "The doc doesn't want you on a horse for a week."

"He's crazy," Horn said. "You know how far ahead of us Sandusky will be by then."

"Sure," Siringo said, "I'm no dummy. A week further than today."

"That's right," Horn said. "You give me a day, maybe two, and we'll get back on their trail."

"We'll see about that," Siringo said. "Right now I'm gonna go and talk to the sheriff."

"What's he got to do with anythin'?"

"He's the local law," Siringo said. "I just wanna fill him in."

"Well, I guess I'll be right here," Horn said.

"I'll get us some hotel rooms and help you get over there later," Siringo said.

"You gonna be around, Adams?" Horn asked.

"I've got noplace to go," Clint said. "I can hang around awhile."

"We'll have a drink," Horn said.

"I'll see you in a little while, Tom," Siringo said.

Horn's face was etched with pain as he said, "I'll be fine."

Siringo and Clint left Dr. Epton's office together. They had gotten directions from the doctor to the sheriff's office and headed over there.

"This sheriff doesn't sound like he'd going to be much use," Clint said.

"That's okay," Siringo said. "The Pinkertons just like their men to stay in touch with local law enforcement."

"So this is definitely as Pinkerton job?" Clint asked.

"Oh, yeah."

"Horn's a Pinkerton now?"

"No," Siringo said, "he's working with me, but not for the agency."

"You paying him?"

"Yeah."

"You must have needed him badly."

"He's the best tracker I know."

They reached the sheriff's office and Clint said, "Well, let's go inside. I'm looking forward to hearing this story."

FOUR

Sheriff Nick Kerwin listened patiently while Siringo told him what happened when he and Tom Horn caught up to the Sandusky gang.

"So basically," the man said, "you're tellin' me Tom Horn rode you right into a trap."

"No, that's not what I'm sayin'," Siringo said. "I'm sayin' Tom tracked them down and found them, but just as they were meeting up with some others."

"So when you found them," Kerwin said, "there were twice as many as you expected."

"Right."

"And they shot the shit out of you."

"Well . . . you could put it that way, I guess," Siringo agreed reluctantly.

"And what do you want me to do about it?"

Clint figured whatever Siringo said to that question, he wasn't going to get much out of this man, just as the doctor had warned. They had found the fiftyish sheriff sitting with his feet up on his desk, and he had removed them only grudgingly to see what they wanted.

"Nothin'," Siringo said. "I'm not askin' you to do anythin'. I'm just lettin' you know what happened in your county."

"And who brought you in?"

"Some hands from the Double-Z found us and were good enough to bring us to the doctor's."

"How bad hurt were ya?"

"I got a scratch, Horn's liable to be laid up awhile."

"Here in town?"

"Where else?" Siringo asked. "I can't move him."

"I hope there ain't no trouble with you fellas," Kerwin said. "I don't need no trouble in my town."

"We don't intend to cause any trouble."

The sheriff looked at Clint, who, up to this point, had not been introduced.

"And you? What's your part in all this?"

"I don't have a part, Sheriff," Clint said. "I'm passing through and heard what happened. Siringo and Horn are both . . . acquaintances of mine, so I thought I'd check in and see what happened."

"And are you stayin' around town, too?"

"I am," Clint said, "for a few days."

"What's your name?"

"Clint Adams."

The sheriff hesitated, then asked, "The Gunsmith?"

"That's right," Siringo said with great satisfaction. "The Gunsmith."

"Aw, look," Kerwin said to Clint, "I really don't want no trouble in town, I just—"

"I'm not lookin' for trouble, Sheriff," Clint said. "I just want to make sure my friends are okay."

"Yeah, but you three in one town at the same time? You don't gotta look for trouble, it'll find you."

"That wouldn't be our fault, would it, Sheriff?" Siringo asked.

"You're not telling us to leave town, are you, Sheriff?" Clint asked.

"Naw, naw," Kerwin said quickly and nervously, "I ain't tellin' ya that. I just . . . don't want no trouble."

Clint knew that what the sheriff wanted was not to have to do any work.

"Well, Sheriff," Clint said, "how about we just promise not to look for any? Would that do?"

"Well," Kerwin said unhappily, "I guess that'll have to do."

FIVE

Outside the sheriff's office, Clint said, "Come on, let me buy you a drink."

"Good, I could use one," Siringo said.

"There's a saloon over there," Clint said, pointing. He had, in fact, just spotted it.

The place was small, with no crowd inside, but it had what they wanted, a bar and a beer.

Once they had a beer each, Clint turned to Siringo and said, "Now tell me what you didn't tell the sheriff."

"About what?"

Clint sipped his beer and regarded Siringo over the top of his mug.

"All right," Siringo said. "The Pinkertons were hired to get rid of some rustlers in Santa Fe County. They sent me. I found out who they were, and recruited Horn to track them. That's all true."

Clint remained silent, waiting.

"Okay," Siringo said. "Harlan Sandusky killed a man named Lew Hancock. Lew was a friend of mine."

"When did this happen?"

"Last month."

"Before or after the Pinks were hired?"

"It happened before we were hired," Siringo said. "I found out about it when I went to Santa Fe."

"So this is personal."

"No," Siringo said, "I'm doin' this because the Pinkertons sent me. But yeah, I do want to see Sandusky pay for killin' Lew."

"Does Horn know about Lew?"

"No," Siringo said, "and I don't wanna tell him."

"He won't hear it from me."

Siringo finished his beer and said, "Thanks. Now let me buy you one."

Clint nodded, set his empty mug down on the bar.

"Let's get a table," Siringo said, and led the way to the back.

Once they'd sat down, Clint asked, "What are you going to do now?"

"I got some choices," Siringo said. "I can wait for Horn to heal and then get back on the trail."

"Or?"

"I can go without him."

"Track them alone?"

Siringo nodded.

"What about the odds?" Clint asked.

"The odds were against me when I started."

"But you and Horn rode into a buzzsaw," Clint said. "There were more of them than you thought. And now they know you're coming."

"They think we're dead," Siringo said. "They won't expect us to be coming again."

"Where are they headed?" Clint asked.

"Not sure," Siringo said. "Maybe Mexico."

"If they think you're dead," Clint said, "maybe they'll go back to Santa Fe to keep rustling."

"That could be," Siringo agreed.

"You've got another option, you know," Clint said.

"What's that?"

"You can take me in place of Horn."

"You?" Siringo asked. "Why would you do that?"

Clint shrugged and said, "I've got nothing else to do. With me, you could leave tomorrow."

Siringo rubbed his jaw.

"I'd have to talk to Horn," he said. "Pay him off. Then we'd have to decide on a price."

"I'm not asking you to pay me."

"I'm sayin' the Pinkertons will pay you."

"I don't really want their money either, Charlie," Clint said. "Just say the word and you've got a partner."

"I appreciate that, Clint," Siringo said. "I really would like to get right back on their trail."

"How many we talking about?"

"We started tracking six," Siringo said. "They easily got a dozen now."

"That many men," Clint said, "they'll be easier to track."

"You're probably right about that." Siringo finished his second beer. "I better go and see how Horn's doin', get us some hotel rooms."

"Yeah, I'll need a room, too, for tonight. Why don't I check us all in while you go see Horn?"

"That works for me," Siringo said, and they both stood and left the saloon.

Just outside the batwing doors they parted company.

"I'll meet you at the hotel," Siringo said.

Clint nodded. Siringo headed for the doctor's office and Clint to the nearest hotel. Neither of them saw Sheriff Kerwin watching them from his window.

SIX

"You ain't leavin' me here," Tom Horn said stubbornly. "I don't mind if Adams comes along. We can use his gun. But I ain't stayin' here."

"Tom," Siringo said, "I've got to get back on their trail as soon as possible."

"Fine," Horn said. "Let me rest up tonight and I'll get on a horse tomorrow."

"You can't," Siringo said. "You'll bleed to death."

"I ain't gonna bleed to death," Horn said. "I'm too damn ornery to die. You get them hotel rooms?"

"Clint is gettin' them now."

"Well, get me over there, then, so I can rest up," Horn said. "Help me off this table."

Siringo helped Horn down, wondering how the man was going to get on a horse when he couldn't even get off the table and stand up by himself.

Clint was standing outside the hotel when Siringo came along, with Horn leaning on him.

"Here are your keys," he said, handing them to Siringo. "You need any more help?"

"No, we got it," Horn said. "I just need to rest tonight. I'll be fine in the morning."

Clint looked at Siringo, who just shrugged.

"Glad to hear you're comin' along, Clint," Horn said, "but like I told Charlie, I ain't stayin' behind."

"I guess it's your decision, Tom."

"I'll get Tom into his room and come back down," Siringo said.

Clint nodded, and sat in a wooden chair in front of the hotel to wait.

When Charlie Siringo came back out, he sat next to Clint.

"He's stubborn," he said. "He's gonna get on a horse if it kills him."

"Like I said, the decision is his."

"If he decides to go, are you still gonna come?" Siringo asked.

"Sure," Clint said. "You'll both still be outnumbered. And you may need help with him."

"He might slow us down."

"Oh," Clint said, "I think if Tom Horn gets himself on a horse, he's not going to slow us down."

"I hope you're right."

"I think I am."

After Siringo left Tom Horn on the bed in his room and went out, Horn got himself to his feet. He almost fell over, but put the weight on his right leg and kept himself up. The doctor had wrapped the thigh wound tight, and Horn thought he'd be able to sit a horse without opening the wound.

He walked to the window to look out, then walked back to the bed. By the time he sat back down on the bed, he was sweating. And hungry. Siringo was supposed to bring him something to eat, and he didn't want to be sweating when that happened.

He got himself back on the bed, with his legs up, and started to get his breath back.

He meant what he said to Siringo, and to Clint Adams. He was going to be back on a horse by tomorrow. No damn bullet was going to keep him from finishing this job, and finding that sonofabitch who shot him.

SEVEN

Before turning in, Clint and Siringo agreed to meet in the lobby in the morning, and have breakfast together. Siringo then went to a nearby café to get something for Horn to eat, and brought it to his room.

"I thought you needed a steak," he said as he entered carrying a tray that was covered by a red-and-white-checkered napkin.

"It's about time," Horn said. "I'm starvin'."

Siringo removed the napkin, revealing a steak-and-potato plate, a knife and fork, with a bottle whiskey lying on its side.

"Ah," Horn said, picking up the bottle, "this'll help, too. Get two glasses."

Siringo walked over to a chest of drawers that had a pitcher, a basin, and two glasses on it. By the time he returned to the bed, Horn was attacking the steak with his knife and fork. He poured two fingers into a glass, handed it to Horn, and the man drained it and held it out for more. Siringo poured two more fingers, then set the bottle aside.

Horn took the second glass of whiskey, but put it next to his plate and continued eating. He had a good appetite.

"How's the leg?" Siringo asked.

"It hurts," Horn said truthfully. "But I'll live."

"Well, I hope so," Siringo said. "We have a lot of work to do."

"You still thinkin' about leavin' without me?" Horn asked.

"I think it's gonna be up to you," Siringo said. "If you can get on a horse, then the three of us will ride out of here tomorrow."

"Clint will still come along?"

"Yes."

"That's good," Horn said. "We can use his gun."

"But if you can't get yourself on a horse tomorrow," Siringo went on, "then I suggest Clint and I leave and you rest a few more days before you follow us."

Horn chewed his steak and thought about that.

"From your point of view, it makes sense," he finally admitted.

"We'll even make it easy for you to follow us," Siringo added.

"That won't be a problem," Horn said, "but let's wait and see what happens in the mornin'."

Siringo was thinking that, come morning, Horn probably wouldn't even be able to get out of bed.

Horn devoured his food, then downed the second glass of whiskey.

"What did you and Clint decide?"

"He and I are gonna meet in the lobby for breakfast," Siringo said. "Then we'll come and check on you. After that, we'll all decide what we're gonna do. I don't wanna leave you behind, Tom, but if it's the best thing for you . . ."

"I get it, Charlie," Horn said. "I get it. My own damned fault for bein' stupid enough to stop a bullet. I want to find the bastard who pulled the trigger."

"If we get them all," Siringo said, "it means we got the one who did it."

"We'll get 'em," Horn said, wincing as he changed position. "Let me have another shot, Charlie."

Siringo poured him another shot, then set the bottle down across the room.

"My room is down the hall," Siringo said. "Scream if you want somethin'."

"Oh, I'll scream," Horn said, sleepily setting the tray aside. He was asleep before Siringo went out the door.

Clint went to his room, marveling at how things had changed over the course of the day. He'd only stopped in Las Vegas to restock, never expected to run into somebody he knew, let alone two. And then to hear that they had been shot up. He was glad to see that Charlie Siringo was all right, and hoped Tom Horn would not be foolish enough to try and mount a horse the next day, not with that wound to his thigh.

Clint, being the kind of friend he was, could not let Siringo continue his hunt of the gang alone—not when he was tracking almost a dozen men. He had no choice but to offer to go along—whether Horn traveled or not.

Clint read from a Mark Twain collection of short stories for a while, then turned in. He heard someone walking down the hall before he went to sleep, then a door closed, and he assumed that it was Siringo. After that, all was quiet.

Siringo went to his own room and peeled off his clothes. He wished he'd had time to take a bath and get some clean clothes, but that wasn't to be. He slapped as much dirt from his clothes as he could, then set them on the wooden chair in the corner.

Whether Horn was ready or not, he intended to ride out of Las Vegas the next morning. He'd meant what he said to Horn. The man could follow after him and Clint when he was ready. He would probably catch up to them before they caught the gang. Hopefully, Sandusky thought they were dead, and would not recruit any more men. Going up against a dozen would be bad enough, but not as daunting as it might have been with Clint Adams along. Among the three of them, Siringo knew they had all the talent to make the perfect Pinkerton. Clint would fill in what Siringo and Horn were missing—a deadly accurate hand with a gun. Siringo and Horn could shoot, but they did not have the talent Clint Adams had.

Siringo slid between the sheets. It felt too good after so many days on the trail, and tomorrow night he'd be back on the hard ground. He didn't know whether to sleep on the floor, or go ahead and enjoy the mattress for the one night. Before he could make up his mind, he fell asleep.

EIGHT

When Clint came down to the lobby the next morning, he found Siringo waiting for him. Charlie was wearing the same clothes he'd had on the day before. He obviously hadn't had a chance to bathe, or buy clean duds.

"How's Horn?" he asked.

"He was okay last night," Siringo said. "Ate a big steak, had a few drinks, then fell right to sleep."

"He's going to be stiff this morning."

"I know," Siringo said, "but I learned a long time ago never to underestimate him. Besides, he's younger than we are."

Both Siringo and Horn were younger than Clint, but Horn was the one who was not yet thirty. Maybe that would work in his favor when it came to healing.

"Let's get some breakfast," Siringo said. "Then we can bring him some eggs and see how he's doin'."

The hotel didn't have a dining room so Siringo took Clint to the same café he had gotten Horn's steak from. The waiter there told him not to worry about the tray; someone from the hotel would bring it back.

They got seated among the other diners. Clint had his usual steak and eggs while Horn went for bacon and eggs. When the waiter set a basket of hot biscuits on the table, they both attacked them.

"Tell me about Sandusky," Clint said.

"He's a hard man," Siringo said. "Forty or so, been on his own a long time. No relatives. He's a killer, and he's crafty. Up to now nobody's been able to catch him."

"We're going to change that," Clint said. "What about his men?"

"He grabs 'em where he can," Siringo said. "The only one who rides with him all the time is a fella named Cal Anderson."

"Don't know him."

"They're friends, been ridin' together since the war," Siringo said.

"That's a long time."

"The others come and go," Siringo said. "Sometimes Sandusky and Anderson just get rid of them."

"Kill them, you mean?"

Siringo nodded.

"When they get tired of sharin' the proceeds of their jobs," Siringo said. "That's what I hear anyway."

"You wonder what makes anybody follow someone like that," Clint said.

"They all think it won't happen to them," Siringo said. "They think they'll get rich and ride away, but a lot of them don't make it in time."

"Who sent you out on this job, Charlie?"

"William."

"Still running the Chicago branch?"

"Pretty much. Him and Robert are runnin' the whole agency."

"How do you think he'll react when he hears about me?" Clint asked.

"I ain't gonna tell 'im," Siringo said. "Not yet anyway. If I do, it'll be after the job is over."

They finished their breakfast and washed it down with a last cup of coffee.

"Okay," Siringo said, "we better go up and see how Horn's doin'."

They got a plate of bacon and eggs, a mug, and a pot of coffee and headed up to Tom Horn's room.

Tom Horn couldn't move.

He woke up lying on his good side, opened his eyes, and looked around. He didn't try to move right away. He felt all right if he lay perfectly still. The next step would be to try to move.

First he used his hand to feel his thigh. It was still wrapped tightly, and as he ran his fingers over the skin, he could feel his fingertips. That was good. The doctor told him to come back if the leg felt numb. Next, he tried to move the injured leg, ended up gritting his teeth at the pain. It was stiff, and it hurt to move, but he flexed it, then flexed it again. It wasn't as bad the second time as the first, so he did it again.

Not too bad.

Next he had to roll onto his back. He did that slowly, and not without some pain, not only in his leg, but also in his back. He felt stiff, but he knew he'd feel that, and he knew he'd feel pain. What he didn't want to do was start bleeding again.

He stayed on his back, staring at the ceiling, catching his breath. There was some sweat on his brow, and he waited for that to cool before he tried anything else.

Next would come sitting and then, finally, standing.

                           *   *   *

Clint carried the tray, and as they got to the door, Siringo
used the key to unlock it. They walked in and stopped short
when they saw Tom Horn on his feet.

"Well, well," Siringo said. "How long did it take you to
stand up?"

"Long enough," Horn said. "I'm just tryin' to walk out
the stiffness."

As if to illustrate his point, he walked across the room,
stiff-legged but steady.

"Looks good," Siringo said. "We brought you some eggs
and bacon."

"Good," Horn said. "I'm hungry."

"Sit on the bed," Clint said.

They watched him carefully as he walked to the bed and
slowly sat down. He kept his weight away from the wounded
thigh. Clint gave him his tray and he started to devour the
eggs and bacon.

"Think you can sit a horse?" Siringo asked.

"I'm gonna try," Horn said. "But just in case . . ."

"Just in case what?" Siringo asked.

"Well, if I start bleeding on the trail, we're gonna have
to rewrap this wound."

"I'll go over to the doc's and get some extra bandages,"
Siringo said.

"Thanks," Horn said. He looked at Clint. "You still
comin'?"

"I'm coming."

"Good," Horn said. "We can walk over to the livery for
the horses."

"You two still got your horses?"

"Yeah," Siringo said, "the same ranch hands who found
us rode 'em down and caught 'em."

Horn popped the last piece of bacon into his mouth and set the tray aside. Clint and Siringo watched him carefully as he got to his feet. He picked up his gun belt and strapped it on.

"Tom," Clint said, "you could bleed to death."

"That's why we're gettin' the extra bandages," Horn said. "If I can sit a horse, boys, I'm ridin' along."

"Okay," Siringo said. "We better get goin'."

The three of them walked out the door and down into the lobby, moving at Horn's pace.

Outside Siringo said, "I'll go to the doc's and meet you at the stable."

"We'll have the horses saddled," Clint said.

NINE

Horn was willing to step aside while Clint saddled the horses, but when it came time to mount, he insisted on doing it himself.

"If I can't even get on," he said, "I've got no business going."

Clint agreed and withdrew his helpful hand.

Horn hesitated, trying to decide how to do it. Normally he put his left leg—the injured leg—into the stirrup, and lifted himself into the saddle. He could have walked around to the other side and mounted using his right leg, but in the end he just went for it. If the wound exploded . . . he might as well find out now.

He put his left leg in the stirrup, grabbed the saddle with both hands, and lifted, taking as much of his weight as he could on his arms. He swung his right leg over, and just like that, he was mounted, and there was no explosion of blood.

"How was it?" Clint asked.

"Surprisingly," Horn said, "not bad."

"Come on," Clint said, "we'll wait for Charlie outside."

* * *

Siringo accepted the extra bandages from the doctor, who also instructed him on the proper way to wrap the leg.

"And put some of this on the wound," he added, handing Siringo a jar of ointment. "It should keep it from becoming infected."

"Thanks, Doc."

"The man's a fool," the doctor said. "Somewhere along the line, he's gonna have to pay for this."

"Well," Siringo said, "we'll help him as much as we can."

"He'll need it."

"Thanks again, Doc."

Siringo settled the bill with the doctor, and headed for the livery stable.

While Horn remained mounted, Clint stood holding the reins of Eclipse and Siringo's horse. The detective appeared, carrying a bundle. They each had some supplies in their saddlebags, which Siringo had purchased the day before.

"How did he get up there?" Siringo asked.

"All by himself," Clint said.

"Well, he ain't fallen off yet, so I guess he's okay."

Siringo walked to his horse and stuffed the bundle into his saddlebag. He took the reins of his horse from Clint and mounted up. Clint walked Eclipse away from the other two and swung himself into the saddle.

"We got everythin' we need?" Horn asked.

"Pretty much," Siringo said.

"Then we better get goin'."

Clint and Siringo both looked at Horn. There was no telling how he'd react to the rigors of riding. Just the bouncing up and down could start him bleeding or, at the very least, cause him pain.

"Tom," Siringo said, "let's just take it easy to start and see how your leg responds. Whataya say?"

"Sure," Horn said, "makes sense."

"Where do we start?" Clint asked.

"Right where they bushwacked us," Siringo said. "We should be able to pick up their trail from there."

"I'll take the lead," Horn said. "That way if I fall off my horse, you'll see me."

TEN

They rode at Horn's pace. Clint figured Horn took the lead because that was where he was accustomed to being, but also so they wouldn't be able to see the expression on his face.

"How's he look to you?" Siringo asked, keeping his voice low.

"He's sitting okay," Clint said. "I guess we'll really find out when we start to ride faster."

"I can hear you both back there," Horn said. "If you got somethin' to say, just say it."

"We was just sayin' you're lookin' good, Tom," Siringo said.

"How do you feel?"

"I'm fine," Horn said. "Just stop mutterin' behind me."

"Yeah, okay," Siringo said.

When they reached the point where Siringo and Horn were bushwacked, Horn remained mounted while Clint and Siringo stepped down.

"This is where they got us," Siringo said.

Clint could still see some blood on the ground. He wondered how much of it belonged to Siringo and Horn.

"Looks like you might have done okay," he said. "There's enough blood to indicate you hit some of them."

"If I know Sandusky," Siringo said, "he's already replaced those men."

Horn was riding his horse in circles, studying the ground.

"Tom?" Siringo yelled.

"I got 'em," Horn said. "Ten, twelve horses. Doesn't look like they left anybody behind."

"Which way are they headed?" Clint asked.

"South."

"South it is," Siringo said.

The detective and Clint mounted up, rode to join Tom Horn.

"I was thinkin' they might go north, back to where they came from, since they thought we was dead, but no."

"Maybe," Siringo said, "they ain't assumin' we're dead."

"Then why didn't they finish us off?"

"I don't know," Siringo said.

"Well then," Horn said, "we should just get started trackin' them. Maybe at some point they'll double back."

"Maybe," Siringo said.

But by the time the sun started to go down, the tracks still had not doubled back. The Sandusky gang was still heading south.

"We better camp here," Siringo said.

"I'm fine," Horn said. "Don't stop on my account."

"I ain't," Siringo said. "It's just time."

They reined their horses in, and Clint and Siringo dismounted first. They both watched as Horn stepped down, and both saw the red stain on his trousers.

"When did that start bleedin'?" Siringo asked.

"What?" Horn touched his thighs, his hand coming away red, then saw the red smear on his saddle. "Damn, I didn't even feel it."

"We better take a look at it," Siringo said. "We'll need a fire."

"I'll see to the fire," Clint said.

"I'll take the horses," Siringo said. "Tom, just settle down somewhere."

"There's a stream," Horn said. "I can get some water."

"Just sit down somewhere," Siringo said. "Don't be a fool and make it any worse."

"Yeah, okay."

Clint got the fire going, and then went and got the water. Siringo got all three horses unloaded, rubbed down, and picketed. Then he carried the saddlebags to the fire.

"You see to Tom's leg," Clint said. "I'll cook."

"I remember that trail coffee of yours," Siringo said. "You could clean your gun with it."

"I'll take it easy," Clint promised.

Siringo walked over to Horn, who had found a boulder to sit on.

"Gotta get them trousers down, Tom," Siringo said.

"Yeah, okay." Horn stood stiffly, undid his gun belt and belt, and lowered his trousers.

Siringo tossed the man's bedroll down and said, "Lie on that."

Horn got down on his stomach and Siringo began to unwrap the bloody bandage. Clint brought over some water so Siringo could clean the wound.

"I didn't realize that bullet took such a chunk out of you, Tom," Siringo said. "Damn, you should be in bed, resting and healing."

"Just do what you can and wrap it," Horn said.

"Okay."

"And then I want to eat."

Siringo cleaned the wound, applied the salve the doctor had given him, then put a clean bandage in place and wrapped it as tightly as he could.

"You got another pair of trousers?" he asked Horn.

"No."

"Damn," Siringo said, "I'll have to go to the stream and do your laundry. You'll have to eat in your skivvies."

"As long as I get to eat."

Horn got himself up again and sat on the boulder, keeping his bandaged leg straight out, with no pressure on the wound.

Siringo went down to the stream and soaked Horn's trousers, trying to get as much of the blood out as he could.

By the time he got back, he could smell the bacon and beans Clint had prepared, and Horn was already working on a plate. Clint handed one to Siringo as he approached the fire.

"How's it look?" Clint asked, referring to Horn's wound.

"Bad," Siringo said, "but I didn't see none of what the doctor said infection would look like."

"Well, that's good anyway."

Clint stuffed some bacon and beans into his mouth as Siringo sipped his coffee.

"Oh, Jesus," the detective said. "You sonofabitch."

"It's good for you," Clint said. "Make a man of you."

"Damn!" Siringo put the cup down between his feet on the ground. Clint knew he'd finish it and ask for more.

"If the gang keeps going south," Clint said, "maybe they're headed for Lincoln County to do some rustling there."

"Could be."

"Although it might be better if they double back."

"Either way," Siringo said, "we'll catch up to them."

"Sounds like this might be personal for you and Horn now."

"Every job is a little personal," Siringo said.

"Yeah, but you don't get shot in every job," Clint said. "Speaking of which, how's your arm?"

"It's fine," Siringo said, picking up his coffee cup. "If it starts to hurt, I can just pour some of this on it. That should take care of any infection."

ELEVEN

Harlan Sandusky looked out the window of his cabin. It was a shack, really, just barely standing. The rest of the men were camped outside, but Sandusky was the leader, so he slept inside.

He stared out the window at his men and knew they were a motley lot. Still, they didn't have to be smart to rustle cattle. That was his part.

He saw his *segundo*, Cal Anderson, walking among the men, talking to some, barking at others. Anderson kept the men in line, and was the only man Sandusky trusted.

He turned and looked at the woman in the room. Delilah West was the only female member of the gang. As such, she was the one who had to make Sandusky the happiest.

She was sitting on his cot, wearing only a pair of jeans. Her feet were bare, and so were her big breasts. Sandusky, who was totally naked, walked up to her, his raging hard cock leading the way. As he approached her, she smiled. She was forty, missing a few teeth, and her face and body were dirty and sweaty. He wished she was prettier, but she wasn't exactly ugly. Maybe just plain. But she had a wide mouth with full lips, and when she wrapped them around his cock, he forgot about pretty or ugly. He reached down to squeeze her breasts and nipples while she sucked him eagerly, holding on to the base of his huge cock with both hands. The shack was eventually filled with wet, sloppy noises.

Sandusky began to growl as he came near to exploding in her mouth, but before that could happen, he grabbed her by the hair and threw her off him. Then he pushed her onto her back and yanked her jeans off her. Once she was naked and he could see that wild tangle of red hair between her legs, he became single-minded. He mounted her on the cot, grabbed her ankles, spread her legs, and drove his hard cock into her, fucked her brutally enough that the men outside could hear her screaming . . .

Later he threw her jeans and torn shirt at her and said, "Get out. I got some thinkin' to do."

"Jesus, Harlan, lemme get dressed at least," she complained.

He grabbed her arm and pushed her toward the door, saying, "Out!"

Battered and bruised—her big brown nipples swollen for more than one reason—she staggered out of the shack even before she could get dressed. The other men eyed her nudity for as long as they could, and then, fully dressed, she approached the group, slapping two or three of them, until one of them tossed her a bottle of whiskey. She opened it with her teeth and guzzled the remains, then laughed . . .

Sandusky, still naked, went back to his coffeepot and poured a cup. While he drank it, he thought about Charlie Siringo being on his trail for the Pinkertons. He wished he'd had time to go back and check to make sure Siringo and his partner were dead, but those ranch hands had heard the shooting and showed up pretty quick. His men were tired and he didn't want to get into a full-scale firefight.

If he knew for sure Siringo was dead, he would have taken his men back to Santa Fe County for some more rustling. However, not knowing for sure, he had to execute another plan. They could go to Mexico and wait for the heat to die down, but that didn't mean they couldn't stop off in Lincoln and grab some more cattle. They could drive them to Mexico and find a buyer there.

His thoughts went back to Siringo. An ex-cowhand turned detective, he turned out to be a damned good one. Charlie Siringo was literally the only man Sandusky was concerned about.

Sure wished he knew for sure if he was dead.

And suddenly he wished he hadn't kicked Delilah out so soon . . .

Clint had taken the last watch, so he had breakfast on the fire when the others woke up.

"Ah, damn it!" Tom Horn growled as he came awake.

"You okay?" Clint asked.

"Oh, yeah," Horn said, "just stiff."

"You need help gettin' to your feet?" Siringo asked, standing.

Horn seemed to give the offer some thought, then said, "Ah, why not?"

Siringo went over and gave Horn a hand. Horn grabbed it and Siringo hauled him carefully to his feet.

"Ahh," Horn groaned as he straightened. He started to walk around a bit, testing his leg. "You musta done a good job, Charlie."

"I hope so," Siringo said.

"Come on over here and have some breakfast," Clint suggested. "Might make you feel even better."

"Not his coffee," Siringo warned.

"What's wrong with his coffee?" Horn asked. "I like it. Good trail coffee."

"Jesus," Siringo said, shaking his head, but he accepted a cup from Clint.

After breakfast Horn decided to pitch in, so he said he'd refill the canteens. Clint broke camp and killed the fire, while Siringo saddled the horses.

They were ready to go.

Horn insisted in mounting his horse on his own, so Clint and Siringo fell back, ready to jump in if he fell. But he managed to get himself in the saddle. Clint and Siringo mounted up, and they started south.

Sandusky pulled on his jeans, then called Anderson into the shack.

"Close the door," he said, not that it made any difference. The windows had no glass, and the walls were so thin, anybody who wanted to listen in could.

"What's up, boss?" Anderson asked. "Man, you sure tore Delilah up, huh? She looks sore as hell."

"I wanna stop over in Lincoln County and get some cows, Cal."

"Where we gonna sell 'em?"

"Mexico."

"We're gonna drive 'em all the way to ol' Mexico?" Anderson asked.

"It ain't that far," Sandusky said, "and we can use the money."

Anderson shrugged and said, "You're the boss."

"You think these men are up to it?" Sandusky asked.

"Most of 'em are," Anderson said. "Skeeter, Nelson, Rosario . . . they're good men."

"All right, then," Sandusky said. "Start breakin' camp and we'll head to Lincoln."

"What do I tell the men?"

"Nothin'," Sandusky said. "They'll find out when the time comes."

"Right."

"Anderson."

"Yeah?"

"I know you got friends out there," Sandusky said, "but don't get too attached, huh?"

Anderson gave a wolfish grin and said, "I getcha, boss."

TWELVE

Suddenly, the trail swung east.

"This is odd," Horn said.

"Where could they be headed?" Clint asked.

"Santa Rosa?" Siringo asked. "It's the biggest town east of here."

"Maybe they want to rest," Clint said.

"Could be," Horn said.

"We got no choice," Siringo said. "We gotta follow."

Horn shrugged and said, "Let's go."

They rode along Santa Rosa Lake later in the day until they came to a cold campsite, with a worn-out shack next to it.

"They stopped here," Horn said, looking around. "Looks like at least overnight, maybe two nights."

"I'll check the shack," Clint said, and rode over to it. He dismounted and went inside.

Horn dismounted on his own, stood there for a moment, then turned and started walking. He was stiff, Siringo could see that, but he wasn't complaining and—more important— he wasn't bleeding.

"I got maybe a dozen horses picketed here," Horn called out.

"Lots of boot scuffs on the rocks here," Siringo said. They weren't going to find many tracks because the ground was hard, but it was well scuffed. He bent over and picked something up. "Cigar butt," he called.

"Lemme see," Horn said, coming over.

Siringo handed it over. Horn smelled it, then tried a few puffs.

"It's dead," he said, "but not long. Probably this mornin'."

"They camped here 'til this mornin'?" Siringo said. "We're less than a day behind?"

"Looks like it."

"Let's see what Clint's got."

They started for the shack.

Inside the shack Clint could see that one man had camped there, probably the leader. There was an old shirt left behind, an empty whiskey bottle, a couple of flattened cigarettes, and burned matches. He touched the wall of the shack, realized it could fall in on him any minute, and got out of there.

"What's inside?" Siringo asked.

"Not much," Clint said. "Looks like the leader kept himself apart from his men."

"Sandusky," Siringo said.

"If it's them."

"It's them," Horn said.

"How can you be sure?"

"The tracks led us here," Horn said. "I recognize some of them. They're pretty distinctive."

"Okay," Siringo said, "then we're just a matter of hours behind."

"Where'd they go from here?" Clint asked. "Santa Rosa?"

"We'll follow the tracks south," Horn said, "but it wouldn't surprise me if they bypass Santa Rosa."

Horn stretched and Clint asked, "How's the leg?"

"I'm fine," Horn said. "Let's get back on their trail."

Horn mounted with seemingly more ease than before. Clint wondered how much effort that actually took.

THIRTEEN

As Horn had opined, the gang bypassed Santa Rosa. Not only that, they swung west.

"Now what?" Clint asked.

"Still going south," Horn said, "but now it's southwest."

"Carrizozo?" Siringo wondered.

"Maybe," Horn said. "It's small, but they can stock up there."

The three men exchanged a glance.

"It's your call, Charlie."

"If they bypassed Santa Rosa, they're gonna need supplies," the detective said. "Carrizozo figures."

"So we can stop tracking them and head straight there?"

Siringo thought about it.

"If we do that and they bypass Carrizozo, we could lose 'em," Horn said.

"We're only a few hours behind," Siringo said. "Let's stay on their trail."

* * *

They followed the trail for the better part of the day. Horn drew his horse to a stop, Clint and Siringo following his lead.

"You okay?" Clint asked.

"I'm fine," Horn said, although his face was very pale beneath his perpetual sunburn. "Looks like we were right. They're headed straight to Carrizozo."

"Can we make it tonight?" Clint asked.

"If we ride in the dark," Horn said.

That didn't sound like a good idea to Clint. All it would take was a small stumble and Horn's horse might unseat him. If that happened, his wound would burst open when he hit the ground.

"Why push it?" Clint asked.

"I was thinkin' the same thing," Siringo said.

"You're both bad liars," Horn said, "but I ain't gonna argue."

As Clint had suspected, Horn's wound was giving him trouble.

"We'll camp and head out first thing in the morning," Siringo said. "If they're in Carrizozo now, we won't be that far behind them."

They made camp. This time Siringo fetched the water and built the fire while Clint picketed the horses. Horn sat down immediately after dismounting, leaning his weight off his injured leg. For the most part he'd been doing pretty well, but if he was going to start slowing them down, they'd have to leave him behind. Maybe in Carrizozo. But Clint figured it was up to Siringo to bring it up.

By the time Clint got to the fire, Siringo had the coffee-pot going, and bacon in the pan.

* * *

When Sandusky and his gang reached Carrizozo, he sent three men to buy supplies while the others waited at the edge of town. A dozen men riding down the main street would attract attention, which he didn't need at the moment. Since the town was the county seat of Lincoln County, they were where they wanted to be, and Sandusky was anxious to get a move on.

While the men were sitting around the campfire eating that evening, Sandusky and Anderson were off to the side.

Sandusky said, "There's a ranch not far from here that usually runs five hundred head or so."

"We can't drive that many to Mexico," Cal Anderson said.

"We don't need five hundred," Sandusky said. "We'll grab a hundred or so."

"What ranch is it?" Anderson said.

"Used to be John Chisum's place," Sandusky said. "Back in the sixties he was running a hundred thousand head."

"Who owns it now?" Anderson asked.

"Don't rightly know, but I hear there's always plenty of cattle there."

"It's gonna slow us down," Anderson said.

"Who do you think is after us?"

"Siringo," Anderson said.

"Yeah," Sandusky said, "but if he's alive, he's alone. One against twelve. I'll take those odds every time."

Anderson didn't look convinced. If Siringo was alive, Horn might be alive, too, even if Anderson himself had put Horn down. He knew he'd hit him at least twice, but he hadn't actually seen him die.

"Don't worry so much, Cal," Sandusky said. "That's my job, remember?"

"Yeah, I remember."

Sandusky slapped his *segundo* on the back and said, "Just enjoy your meal. Tomorrow we'll pick up some cows and head for Mexico."

"It's a long way," Anderson said.

"It'll be worth it," Sandusky told him, "when we get there."

FOURTEEN

Clint had a decent pot of coffee ready when Siringo and Horn woke the next morning.

"I knew I wouldn't get away from this for long," Siringo said, but he drank a cup. At the very least, it was eye-opening.

Horn rolled over and struggled to his feet, accepted a cup from Clint.

"No breakfast," Clint said. "We'll have to buy some more supplies in Carrizozo. Maybe get a doctor to look you over."

"I won't argue with that," Horn said.

They broke camp, Clint dousing the fire and Siringo saddling the horses. This time Horn took some assistance in getting in the saddle.

They headed for Carrizozo.

The trail led right to the edge of town, where it got lost among other tracks leading into town. No matter, they could pick it up again on the other side.

Twelve men riding into Carrizozo would have been noticeable. All they had to do was ask.

"I'll talk to the local law," Siringo said. "You get Tom to a doctor."

"Right," Clint said. "Let's meet at the mercantile."

"Okay," Siringo said.

They split up.

Siringo entered the sheriff's office. There was a time when Pat Garrett would have been there, but since killing Billy the Kid, Garrett had written a book about it and had moved on to Texas, where he was the captain of a company of Texas Rangers.

The present sheriff of Lincoln County looked up from his desk as the detective entered. He was a mild-looking bald man in his fifties.

"Help ya?" he asked.

"Charlie Siringo," Siringo said, "Pinkerton Agent, Sheriff . . ."

"Hapwell," the man said, "George Hapwell. I know who you are, Mr. Siringo. What brings you to Lincoln County?"

"I'm tracking a gang of rustlers," Siringo said, "and have reason to believe they rode through here as recently as yesterday."

"Rustlers?" Hapwell asked. "Through here? How many men are we talkin' about?"

"At least a dozen," Siringo said.

"Sir, if a dozen men had ridden into this town yesterday," Hapwell said, "I would know about it."

"So you're sayin' they didn't come through town?"

"They did not."

"Their trail leads right to the edge of town."

"I don't know what to tell you," Hapwell said. "A dozen men did not ride into this town yesterday, or in the past week."

* * *

Clint found the doctor's office, helped Horn down off his horse, and took him inside.

"Can I help you gents?" a short, straw-haired man asked.

"Are you the doctor?" Clint asked.

"I am."

"You're a little young," Horn observed.

The doctor studied Horn and said, "Probably only a year or two younger than you. However, if one of you needs a doctor, I'm what you've got."

"This man was shot several days ago," Clint said, "and against his doctor's orders, he's been riding. We'd like you to take a look at the wound."

"Of course," the doctor said. "Step through that door, please."

Clint helped Horn through the door and onto an examining table. The doctor followed them.

"I can take it from here," he said to Clint.

"I'll be outside," Clint replied. "Thanks, Doc."

As soon as he left the room, the doctor closed the door.

"Okay," Siringo said, "so a dozen men didn't ride into town. Have any strangers been through town?"

"Well," Hapwell said, "now that you mention it, three men did ride into town yesterday."

Siringo wondered if the sheriff was really this stupid.

"And did they stay overnight?"

"No," Hapwell said, "they went to the mercantile, and then left."

"So they were in town for . . ."

"Maybe an hour."

"And you knew about this how?"

"I happened to be in the mercantile at the time."

"So you know what they bought?"

"Some supplies," Hapwell said. "I don't know exactly what. You'd have to talk to Wendell Court. He owns the store."

"Thank you, Sheriff."

"Do you think those were your men?"

"Some of them."

"So where do you think the others went?" Hapwell asked.

"Probably just waited outside of town."

"I hope you catch up with them."

"Yeah, Sheriff," Siringo said, "so do I. Thanks for your help."

"Sure," Hapwell said. "Let me know if there's anythin' else I can do while you're in town."

"I will."

"Any idea how long that might be?" Hapwell asked as Siringo walked to the door.

"No, idea," Siringo said. "I have a friend seein' your doctor, but I'm hopin' not overnight."

He left the office before the sheriff could ask another question.

FIFTEEN

The doctor came out and addressed Clint.

"Well, there's no infection," he said. "That's good. He shouldn't be riding, but on the other hand, he hasn't done any lasting damage to himself—not yet anyway."

"Then he can continue to ride?"

"That's going to be up to him," the doctor said, "if he wants to take the chance that he will do some damage eventually."

"Well, if I know him," Clint said, "he'll want to take the chance."

"His choice," the doctor said. "What about you? Anything ailing you?"

"Me? I'm fine," Clint said. "No, this was just for Tom."

"Okay, then," the doctor said. "He should be dressed by now, but he might need help getting down from the table."

"Okay, thanks."

Clint went into the room just as Horn was trying to get down.

"Here, let me give you a hand," he said, rushing to Horn's side.

"Thanks."

With Clint's aid, Horn managed to stand up without falling down.

"The doctor gave me a clean bill of health," Horn said.

"Kinda," Clint added.

"Whataya mean?"

"He left it up to you, I know," Clint said. "You can ride if you want to."

"I'll ride as long as I can," Horn said. "When I fall off, you can leave me where I lay."

"We'll see about that," Clint said.

"Where's Charlie?"

"Talking to the sheriff," Clint said. "We're supposed to meet him at the mercantile."

"Let's do that, then," Horn said, "and maybe after that we can get a drink."

"Sounds good to me," Clint said.

They settled with the doctor and left the man's office.

SIXTEEN

When they reached the mercantile, Siringo was standing at the counter, paying for supplies. A drink sounded good to him, too, so they stuffed their purchases into their saddlebags and crossed the street to a saloon.

The saloon was about half full, with plenty of room at the bar. They lined up and Clint ordered three beers.

Horn drank down half of his quickly with his eyes closed.

"Ahh," he said, "I needed that."

"I think you might need more than that," Clint said.

"Whataya mean?"

"You need rest, Tom."

"I think he's right," Siringo said.

"I can rest after we catch Sandusky and his crew," Horn said defensively. "Unless you think I ain't pullin' my weight."

"That ain't it at all, Tom," Siringo said. "Even if you're only half the man you usually are, you're twice as good as anyone else."

That seemed to mollify Horn a bit.

"Then if it's all right with you two, I'll just keep on and rest when we're done."

"It's okay with me," Clint said. "The decision is yours."

"Yeah, okay," Siringo said. "Have it your way."

"Let's get another beer before we move," Horn suggested.

"Do we want to spend the night?" Clint asked, thinking of Horn's leg.

Siringo decided not to coddle Horn, if that was what the man wanted.

"We can't afford to," Siringo said.

"Okay, so what did the sheriff say?"

"That if twelve men had ridden into his town yesterday, he'd know it."

"So they didn't?" Horn asked.

"Not accordin' to him."

"You believe him?" Clint asked.

"I'm not sure," Siringo said. "But he did say three men rode in, and rode out after going to the mercantile."

"Did you ask the clerk there if he knew anythin'?" Horn asked.

"I did," Siringo said, "and I'm convinced that once I left there, he couldn't have described me a minute later."

"So then let's assume the gang sent three men in to do their shopping, and then moved on," Clint said.

"Which means they must've circled the town," Horn said. "I propose we go back to where we lost their tracks and see if I can pick them up again."

"Agreed," Siringo said.

They got their second beers just as three men entered through the batwings and looked their way.

"See, I told you," one of them said. "Tom Horn."

"You was right," a second man said.

The third man just glared.

"You know them?" Siringo asked in a low tone.

"I think so," Horn said. "Might be the Monroe brothers."

"And?" Clint asked.

"I might have had occasion to kill their brother last year."

"Here?" Siringo asked. "You been here before?"

"No," Horn said, "up north, near Taos."

"They don't look happy," Clint said.

"Horn!" one of them yelled. "You know who we are?"

"Not really," Horn said, standing with his beer mug in his left hand, his right hand free. Clint and Siringo had adopted the same stance.

"Tell yer friends to move away," the spokesbrother said. "We're gonna kill ya."

"Gonna be up to them if they want to move away," Horn said.

"If they get hurt, ain't gonna be our fault."

"Which one are you?" Horn asked.

"I'm Josh," the man said. "This here's Dal and that's Ed. You killed our brother Jess last year, up Taos way."

"The way I recall," Horn said, "he was askin' for it—much the same way you fellas are now."

"That don't matter," Josh said. "You killed Jess, and we gotta kill you. We promised our ma."

"Can I make a suggestion?" Clint asked.

"What?" Josh asked.

"Do you think your ma would want to lose all her boys?"

"You sayin' you're takin' his part?" Josh asked.

"If he ain't sayin' that," Siringo piped up, "I am."

"Who the hell are you?" Josh asked.

"Oh, sorry," Horn said, "I didn't introduce my friends. "This here's Charlie Siringo, and that's a fella named Clint Adams."

"Clint Adams?" Josh asked.

"Clint Adams?" Ed echoed. "The Gunsmith?"

"That's right," Horn said.

"And that's Siringo," Dal Monroe said.

"I heard 'em," Josh growled.

"What are we gonna do, Josh?" Ed asked.

"Shut up!"

"That's a good question, Josh," Horn said. "How do you wanna do this? In here or outside?"

"Three against three?" Josh asked.

"Pretty even, huh?" Siringo asked.

"I don't think so," Josh said. He pointed his finger at Horn. "We'll see you again when you ain't got your gunnies with you."

"I hope not," Horn said, "for your sake."

The Monroes backed out of the saloon. When they hit the boardwalk, their footsteps could be heard hurrying away.

The rest of the men in the saloon were staring at the trio now, aware that Clint Adams, Charlie Siringo, and Tom Horn were in their midst.

"We better go," Clint said, "before somebody gets brave."

"Good idea," Horn said.

They set their unfinished second beers down and headed for the doors. They stepped out, mindful of the fact that the Monroes might be lying in wait for an ambush—but they weren't.

Outside Siringo said, "Gunnies?"

"Ain't you ever been called a gunhand before?" Horn asked.

"Not to my face anyway," Siringo said.

SEVENTEEN

Clint, Siringo, and Horn managed to ride out of town without any trouble. They reached the point where the Sandusky gang's tracks mixed in with others, then they circled around to the other edge of town until Horn picked up the trail again. Clint and Siringo followed behind, letting the man do what he did best.

"There it is," Tom Horn said, pointing at the ground. "They seem to be heading to Lincoln."

About an hour later Horn reined in, Clint and Siringo doing the same behind him.

"They're still heading south," the tracker said.

"Mexico," Clint suggested.

"Eventually," Siringo said, "but Lincoln first."

Clint gave Siringo a surprised look.

"You think they're going to hit a ranch in Lincoln?" he asked. "Having some cattle with them will slow them down."

"It's what they do," Siringo said. "If they think I'm dead

and nobody's on their trail, why not stop and make a few extra dollars?"

"Sounds right to me," Horn said.

"Let's stay on their trail," Siringo said. "They could be heading to one of the bigger ranches."

"Okay," Clint agreed, "this is your show, Charlie. Let's move."

Sandusky looked down at the ranch that spread out beneath them. Anderson sat his horse next to him. The rest of the men were behind.

"There you go," Sandusky said, pointing. "Plenty to pick from."

"Are you really sure about this, Harlan?" Anderson asked.

"Stop worryin', Cal," Sandusky said. "When have I ever been wrong?"

Anderson didn't answer, but if Charlie Siringo was still alive, then Sandusky was wrong now! That meant he could be wrong again.

"When we gonna hit 'em?" Anderson asked.

"It's gettin' dark," Sandusky said, looking at the sky, "Let's hit 'em at first light, before they have a chance to wake up."

"I'll tell the others."

Anderson rode back to the other men while Sandusky remained where he was. He was thinking about Charlie Siringo. If the detective was not already dead, he was hoping he *would* catch up to them so Sandusky could kill him, once and for all.

"Gettin' dark," Siringo said.

"They can't be that far ahead," Horn said. "If we keep goin'—"

"I don't want to ride in the dark," Siringo said, shaking his head.

"Because of me?" Horn demanded. "You think I'm gonna fall off my horse?"

"Because of the horses," Siringo said. "I don't want one of them steppin' into a chuck hole. The last thing we need is a horse with a broken leg, Tom."

"I agree," Clint said. "If we're that close, we can catch them in the morning."

"Fine," Horn said, looking at Siringo. "It's your call."

They made camp, started a fire, had a dinner of bacon and beans they had purchased in Carrizozo.

They sat around the fire, Horn leaning to one side to favor his injured leg.

"You think we got anybody followin' us?" Siringo asked.

"Like who?" Horn asked.

"Like the Monroe brothers?" Clint asked.

"You think those three idiots are gonna come after us?"

"They're out for revenge for their dead brother," Siringo said. "They're not gonna give up that easy."

"I don't think they want to go back home and tell their mother what happened," Clint offered.

"Well," Horn said, "as far as I can tell, there ain't nobody behind us."

"I'll take the first watch," Clint said. "Just to make sure."

"I'll go next," Siringo said. "Is there any more coffee left?"

"I thought you didn't like my coffee," Clint said, lifting the pot.

"Just pour," Siringo said, holding out his cup. "I'll take what I can get."

They moved around after that, Horn rolling himself up in his bedroll with some effort, trying to get comfortable on the ground.

Siringo got his own bedroll ready, but then came back to the fire. Clint handed him another cup of coffee, then set to making a new pot.

"Damn you," Siringo said. "I think I'm gettin' used to this stuff."

"I told you, it's good for you," Clint said, putting the pot back on the fire.

Siringo hunkered down and drank his coffee.

"Something on your mind?" Clint asked.

"Nope," Siringo said, "I just wanted another cup before I turn in." But he looked over his shoulder at Horn, leading Clint to believe there was, indeed, something on this mind.

Finally he said, "Yeah, all right, I'm worried about Horn."

"What about him?"

"When we catch up to the gang, we're gonna be outnumbered," Siringo said. "If Tom was not injured, I wouldn't worry about it so much. But the way he is . . . well, I don't know."

"Look, Charlie," Clint said, "Tom's a grown man, he can make up his own mind. And if we get into a firefight with twelve men and you're worried about him, you're going to get yourself killed."

"Yeah, you're right, Clint," Siringo said. "I know that."

"So just get yourself some sleep and we'll come up with a plan in the morning."

"Yeah, okay, that works." Siringo had a last sip, then threw the remnants into the fire, which flared up. "G'night."

Watching Siringo wrap himself up in his bedroll, Clint hoped it wasn't going to be *him* getting killed because he was worried about the both of them.

EIGHTEEN

Tom Horn stood the last watch and woke Clint and Siringo in the morning.

"Coffee's on," he announced. "Come on, we gotta get goin' before they get too far ahead of us."

"Okay, okay," Clint grumbled, "I'm up."

Siringo rolled out and got his feet without complaint. They all had coffee and then went about breaking camp and saddling the horses.

"We're gonna have to pick up the pace today, Tom," Siringo said to Horn when the horses were ready. Horn knew what he meant. They were going to have to push everyone harder, the horses and themselves.

"I'm ready," Horn said. "Let's catch up to those bastards today."

"Okay," Siringo said, "but we've got to know what we're gonna do when we do catch 'em."

"Whataya mean?" Horn said. "We're gonna take 'em down."

"There's gonna be at least twelve of them, Tom," Clint

said. "Just how do you suggest we take twelve of them down?"

"By surprise."

"And how do you think three of us are going to surprise twelve of them?" Clint asked.

"Ambush," Horn said right away, like he had all the answers.

That didn't sit right with Clint. No matter who he was hunting, he felt no one ever deserved to be shot from an ambush.

"I can't do that," Clint said.

"Why not?" Horn asked.

"Shooting anybody in the back just goes against the grain."

"You mean after all these years of killin' men, you're gettin' religion?" Horn asked.

"Religion's got nothing to do with it," Clint said. "Nobody deserves to be shot in the back." He let the comment about him killing so many men go for now. It had always been his contention—even before his friend Wild Bill was killed by a coward from behind—that shooting somebody in the back was wrong.

Horn looked to Siringo for support.

"Sorry, Tom," the detective said, shaking his head. "I agree. Shooting somebody—anybody—from ambush? That's just murder."

"You've both killed men before," Horn argued. "Why so antsy about it now?"

"I only killed when they were trying to kill me," Clint said.

"Same here," said Siringo.

Horn stared at them.

"I'm surprised you two have managed to live this long," he said finally. "Okay, so what do you propose that we do?"

"Divide and conquer," Clint said.

"Huh?" Horn said.

"Instead of tryin' to take them all at once," Siringo said, "we try to take them a few at a time."

"How do we do that?"

"Well, that's what we've got to figure out," Siringo said.

Once they were back on the trail, Horn predicted they were going to catch up to the Sandusky gang within hours, so they really needed to come up with a strategy by then.

They had no idea how things were going to change.

NINETEEN

Harlan Sandusky watched as his men followed his instructions.

Below them were three wranglers working with about a hundred head of cattle. They were probably driving them to a place where they would join with the majority of the herd.

Sandusky intended for them never to get there.

He sent half a dozen of his men down to grab the cattle, and dispose of the hands. The simplest and easiest way was for them to get as close as possible, and then start shooting.

Just in case that started the hundred head stampeding, he had placed the rest of his men so that they'd be able to intercept the small herd and stop them before they really got started. Delilah remained at his side.

He and Anderson watched the action, making sure that everything went right.

It did.

The three ranch hands were dead before they knew what

happened. The cows did panic and start to run, but the rest of the men successfully cut them off and stopped them.

Sandusky and Anderson rode down to where the nine men were sitting their horses, surrounding the cows.

"Cal, better check those wranglers," Sandusky said.

"Right."

Sandusky rode around the small herd, examining the beeves.

"Where we gonna sell 'em, boss?" one man asked.

"Mexico."

"We gonna drive these cows all the way to ol' Mexico?" another man asked, surprised. "What if they send a posse after us?"

"You know a posse we couldn't take care of?" Sandusky asked. "Don't worry about that."

"Harlan knows what he's doin'," Delilah chimed in.

But the men *were* worried. Driving a hundred head to Mexico didn't sound possible to them—not without getting caught.

Anderson came riding up and said, "They're all dead, Harlan."

"Good," Sandusky said. "That'll send a message. Won't be too many volunteers for a posse after they see this. They do manage to get a posse together, ain't gonna be much of one."

"Where to now?" Anderson asked.

"South," Sandusky said, "we just keep on goin' south. And keep these cows tight. I don't wanna lose any of 'em." He stood up in his stirrups. "Move 'em out!"

Three hours later Clint, Siringo, and Tom Horn rode up to a ranch house where a group of men were gathered.

"Uh-oh," Siringo said.

"Looks like they hit already," Clint said.

"I don't like the way this looks," Horn said. "We should get out of here."

"Uh-uh. We've got to find out what happened," Siringo said.

"That looks like a lynch mob to me," Tom said, pointing.

"They don't lynch people for stealin' cattle," Siringo said. "Come on, we'll be okay. Besides, I can prove who I am."

Horn looked at Clint, who shrugged, and the three men rode for the ranch house.

"They don't lynch men for stealin' cattle," Tom Horn repeated to Siringo twenty minutes later. "Is that what you said?"

"Shut up."

Clint, Siringo, and Horn were sitting their horses with their hands tied behind them. They had no sooner ridden up to the group of men than they were set upon, disarmed, and tied. The men did not even give them a chance to say their piece.

"You men are making a big mistake," Clint said.

"Shut up!" someone yelled. "You killed three good men and you're gonna hang for it!"

"It wasn't us!" Siringo chimed in. "We're huntin' the men who did it."

"Yeah, sure."

"If we did it," Siringo asked, "why would we come ridin' back?"

"Who knows what killers do?" somebody asked.

"Aw, hell," somebody else said, "here comes the sheriff."

"Quick," someone said, "hang 'em."

But there was no way they could get the nooses around the necks of Clint, Siringo, and Horn before the man with the badge rode up to them and reined in.

"What the hell is goin' on?" he demanded.

"We're hangin' some no good murderin' rustlers, Sheriff!"

"No, you're not," the lawman said. "Get 'em down off them horses!"

Grumbling, three men stepped forward and eased Clint, Siringo, and Horn off their horses.

"Thank God, Sheriff," Siringo said. "These men were makin' a big mistake."

"That remains to be seen," the sheriff said. "Who are you men?"

"My name's Charlie Siringo," Siringo said. "I'm trackin' those rustles for the Pinkertons."

"You got some proof you're a Pinkerton?" the sheriff asked.

"In my saddlebags."

The lawman walked to Siringo's horse, went into his saddlebags, and came out with his credentials.

"Aw, for Chrissake!" he groaned. "Untie them. You men are idiots!"

"How was we supposed to know he was a Pinkerton?" someone shouted.

"Maybe by askin' him who he was?" the lawman said. "Maybe by checking his bona fides before you hung him? How about that?"

Clint, Siringo, and Horn had their hands cut free.

"Give 'em back their guns."

They accepted their guns and holstered them.

"Well, Mr. Pinkerton," the sheriff said, "who are your friends?"

"Tom Horn," Horn said.

"Clint Adams," Clint added.

The lawman hesitated a moment, then said, "Aw, jeez . . ."

TWENTY

The sheriff introduced himself as Art Delman, and took Clint, Siringo, and Horn into the house.

"The rustlers grabbed about a hundred head," he said, "and killed three men—two wranglers and Andrew Lancer, who owned this spread."

"The owner was out wrangling strays himself?" Siringo asked.

"He liked to work his spread," Delman said. "The rustlers probably thought they were just three cowhands. They didn't realize they were killing an important man hereabouts."

"You got a posse together?" Horn asked.

"Not yet."

"Why not?" Siringo asked.

"Well, we didn't find the bodies for a while," Delman said. "It took a while for the other hands to miss their boss and go lookin' for him. And then they had to send for me."

"And while they were waitin'," Horn said, "they figured they'd string up three strangers."

"They got carried away," Delman said. "Without some-body to tell 'em what to do, they just made the wrong decision."

"You bet they did!" Horn said. "We been trackin' these rustlers a long time, and now these fellas have held us up. We coulda caught up to them today."

"You think so?" Delman asked.

"Now that they've got some cattle with them," Siringo said, "we know so."

"It's still gonna take me some time to get up a posse," Delman admitted. "After another hour or so these men will start to think about their dead comrades, and I won't get so many volunteers."

"So what?" Horn asked. "You want us to do your job for you?"

"Seems to me you'd be doin' your own jobs," the lawman said.

"You wanna come with us, then?" Horn asked.

The lawman was a tall, lanky fellow in his early forties, wore his gun like a schoolteacher would, much too high.

"I don't think so," he said. "I've got to stay here and . . . keep an eye on things."

"Yeah . . . that's what I thought," Horn said.

Horn's tone didn't seem to ruffle the lawman.

"You may think I'm scared or somethin', but I've got responsibilities here."

"Of course you do," Siringo said.

The sheriff studied the detective for a moment, probably trying to figure out if he was being serious or sarcastic.

"I think we've been delayed long enough, Sheriff," Clint said. "We better get going, unless you have something else you can tell us about the rustlers."

"I think I told you all I can."

Clint, Siringo, and Horn exchanged glances, nodded, and headed for the front door. The sheriff followed.

Outside the lynch mob was still gathered, and they watched while the three men mounted their horses.

"Bunch of brave men when they're lynching three innocent strangers," Horn commented. "Won't none of them volunteer for a posse."

"That just means they won't be gettin' in our way," Siringo said.

Horn nodded and said, "I guess that's one way of lookin' at it."

TWENTY-ONE

Sandusky and his crew made good time pushing the hundred head. The cows were well behaved, and his men knew how to handle them.

"We're makin' good time," he commented to Anderson.

"Still too slow, if there's a posse after us," Anderson said nervously.

"Don't worry about a posse," Sandusky said. "I got a plan."

"When do I get to hear it?"

Sandusky looked around them to make sure they could not be overheard. Delilah was sitting at his feet, but she wouldn't dare say a word to anyone. She knew he'd kill her if she did.

"You, me, and Delilah, we're gonna ride on up ahead," he said. "We'll meet up with the men and the cattle in ol' Mexico."

"What if they don't make it to Mexico?" Anderson asked. "What if the posse catches up to them, and . . ."

Anderson trailed off as he noticed Sandusky watching

him with a small smile on his face. Delilah was also smiling.

"Oh, I get it," Anderson said, "I get it."

"If they make it, fine," Sandusky said, "we'll sell the cows. If they don't make it . . ." He stopped and shrugged.

"I get it," Anderson said again.

"See?" Sandusky said. He slid a hand down and into Delilah's shirt until he was cupping one of her big breasts. "I told you to leave the thinkin' to me."

After a few miles Tom Horn was still fuming about the treatment they'd received.

"Goddamned idiots!" he swore.

"Take it easy, Tom," Siringo said.

"It's bad enough we got shot," Horn went on, "but those blamed idiots were gonna hang us! And I bet they think we're gonna bring back their blamed cows!" He looked at Siringo. "We ain't, are we?"

"No," Siringo said. "I ain't interested in savin' their cows. I want Sandusky and his men."

Clint was studying the ground.

"They'll sure be easy to spot," he said. "Why would Sandusky take the chance of grabbing a hundred more cows? Makes them so much easier to track."

All three men reined in and looked at one another.

"Are you thinkin' what I'm thinkin'?" Siringo asked them.

"Sonofabitch," Clint said.

"I ain't no great thinker," Horn said, "but this stinks even to me."

"Sandusky is tryin' to distract us," Siringo said.

"If I was him," Clint said, "I'd let my men drive the cattle and ride up ahead of them. Hell, I'd just head to Mexico."

"So what do we do?" Horn asked. "Head straight for Mexico?"

"It's up to Charlie," Clint said. He and Horn both looked at the detective.

Siringo stood in his stirrups and stretched.

"I'm open to suggestions."

"Is there a time limit on this?" Clint asked.

"Whataya mean?" Siringo asked.

"I mean do you have to catch Sandusky by a certain day?"

"No," Siringo said. "Nobody said nothin' about that. Just catch him."

"And his men, right?" Clint asked. "Not just him, but all of them?"

"All of 'em."

"Then I say we just keep on going the way we're going," Clint said. "If we catch up to his men and he's not with then, they'll be without leadership and easier to take."

"And after we catch 'em," Horn said, "we can let 'em know that Sandusky left them as bait while he ran to Mexico."

"One of them is bound to tell us where they're supposed to meet him."

Clint and Horn remained silent, waiting for Siringo to make the final decision.

"Okay, then," the detective said, "we'll stay on their trail. How far behind are we, Tom?"

"A few hours," Horn said, "but we should be able to close that gap quick. They ain't movin' all that fast."

"Course not," Siringo said. "Sandusky probably told them not to worry about a posse, or about me, because me and Tom are dead."

They started riding again.

"You think he'll take anybody with him to Mexico?" Clint asked.

"Anderson," Siringo said. "They been ridin' together a long time."

"So that leaves ten men driving those hundred head," Clint said.

"That's good," Tom Horn said. "We already cut the odds."

TWENTY-TWO

"You want us to what?" Rosario asked.

"Drive the cows to Mexico while we ride on ahead," Sandusky said.

The Mexican looked at Anderson, who shrugged, then back at Sandusky.

"And you want me to lead them."

"Yeah."

"Porque?" he asked. "Why?"

"Why not?" Sandusky said. "You know your way around Mexico. With you leadin' them, they won't get lost."

"And what will you be doin'?"

"Makin' arrangements to sell 'em when you get 'em there."

Rosario got a crafty look on his face.

"Will I be gettin' a bigger cut if I do this?" he asked.

"A bigger cut?"

"If I am to lead men, I believe I should be paid to lead men, no? *Es verdad?*"

"Okay," Sandusky said, "sure, why not? More money for Rosario." He looked at Anderson. "Remind me."

"Sure, boss."

All three of them looked over to where the other men were tending to the cows.

"We should go and tell them that I am the new *jefe*, eh?"

"Yeah," Sandusky said, "we should definitely do that."

The men did not react well to Rosario being put in charge, but when they raised their voices to protest, Sandusky shouted them all down.

"Does anybody else here know his way around Mexico?" he demanded.

"I been there," a man named Rizzo said.

"Yeah," Sandusky said, "once, when you got drunk in El Paso and wandered across the border. No, Rosario knows his way around, and he's gonna to be in charge until you all reach Mexico." He looked at Rosario. "And then I'm in charge again. Got it?"

"I got it, *jefe*," Rosario said.

"Good," Sandusky said, "then Cal and me and Delilah will get movin', and you boys follow us and get there as soon as you can."

"Why's Delilah get to go?" somebody asked.

"Anybody else willin' to let me stick my dick in your mouth?" Sandusky demanded.

Nobody stepped up.

Delilah smirked.

Rosario's chest was all puffed up as he strutted around, giving orders.

"Let's get out of here," Sandusky said.

When they were out of earshot and sight of the rest of the men, they slowed to a trot.

"That ain't gonna work out, boss," Anderson said. "Those men ain't gonna give Rosario the respect of a leader."

"That's because he ain't a leader," Sandusky said. "He's a damn Mex."

"So they're gonna be totally confused," Anderson said.

"Oh, yeah."

Anderson looked at Sandusky, who was staring straight ahead. There was a look of total satisfaction on his face. Riding beside him, Delilah was grinning broadly, revealing the gaps where her missing teeth used to be.

"Harlan," Anderson said, "I'm kinda glad we been ridin' together as long as we been."

"We been ridin' together too long for me ever to do somethin' like that to you, Cal," Sandusky assured him. "But for the rest of them? There comes a time you gotta use whatever you got to get away. There's always a chance Rosario and the others would kill members of a posse, or Siringo if he ain't already dead."

"And at the very least, they'll slow anyone who's trackin' us down."

"You got it."

"So we ain't gonna look for somebody to buy them cows?"

"No, no," Sandusky said. "We are. Just in case they do make it to Mexico with those cows, I want to be able to sell 'em."

Anderson shook his head.

"You got everythin' covered, don't ya?" Anderson asked.

"He always does," Delilah said.

"I try, Cal," Sandusky said, "and that's what makes a good leader."

TWENTY-THREE

Tom Horn's face was drawn and pale.

"Tom—" Siringo said, but Horn cut him off before he could go any further.

"I'll be fine," Horn said. "They're just ahead of us a bit."

"How can you tell?" Clint asked.

Horn looked at him.

"I can hear the cattle," Horn told them. "And smell 'em."

Clint looked at Siringo, who simply smiled, meaning this was part of the reason he had recruited Tom Horn for the job.

"I think the two of you should stay here while I check," Horn said.

"Okay," Siringo said, "but don't you dare fall off your horse while you're on your own."

"Don't worry, I won't," Horn said.

He rode off ahead of them. Clint and Siringo stepped down from the saddle and opened their canteens.

"He can smell them?" Clint asked. "I can't smell or hear a thing."

"That's why he's the best."

"You think he'll stay in the saddle?"

"I don't think he'll give in to that injury until we catch Sandusky," Siringo said.

They found a couple of rocks to sit on. There wasn't much for the horses to graze on, but the animals managed to find some weeds.

"You know," Siringo said, "you didn't sign on to ride way the hell into Mexico. I'll understand if you wanna turn back."

"I didn't sign on for any of this," Clint said. "I offered to help, and that's what I'm going to do. I'll see this through to the end."

"Appreciate that, Clint," Siringo said. "I think havin' your gun along really evens up the odds for me and Horn against the whole gang."

"Yeah, I know," Clint said. "We got them right where we want them."

Siringo laughed. The two men touched canteens and drank.

They both heard a horse returning and stood up to watch Horn ride back.

"They're up ahead, maybe a mile," Horn said.

"How many?"

"Looks like nine or ten."

Siringo punched the air and said, "We had it figured right. Sandusky and Anderson have ridden on ahead to Mexico."

"All right," Clint said, "what are they doing right now?"

"Arguin'."

"What?" Siringo asked.

"That's what it looks like they're doin'," Horn said. "Arguin', fightin' with each other. The cows are just millin' around."

"Anybody on watch?" Siringo asked.

"Nobody," Horn said. "Right now they're mostly standin' around yellin' at each other. A few of them are on horse-back."

Clint and Siringo exchanged a glance and the detective said, "Sounds perfect."

"Let's go have a look," Clint said.

They mounted up and followed Horn for just about a mile, when he pointed ahead.

"Down there," he said.

"We should go on foot," Siringo said.

"It don't matter," Horn said. "They won't see us 'til it's too late. In fact, you can hear 'em from here."

They fell silent and both Siringo and Clint could hear the raised voices.

"Let's go," Siringo said.

TWENTY-FOUR

In the end they decided that Clint and Siringo would use the cattle for cover and get closer on foot to the outlaws. If they could catch them by surprise, maybe they could take them with a minimum of risk, and blood. Horn would remain mounted and cover them from higher ground with his rifle.

They tied their horses off and circled around the herd. They could still hear the men arguing . . .

"I don't care what Sandusky said," one of the men was shouting, "you ain't no leader."

"Well, I am today, *cabron*," Rosario said. "Now get on those horses and tend to the herd."

"We ain't doin' what you say," another man said.

Skeeter, who wondered why he or Nelson weren't put in charge, said, "Now listen. Sandusky put Rosario in charge. We gotta—"

"We ain't gotta do nothin'," another voice said. "If we follow Rosario, we're all gonna end up dead."

"Or lost," still another voice chimed in.

Rosario put his hand on his gun, which caused the other men to do the same, and they were just seconds from shooting each other . . .

Clint wondered if they shouldn't wait and see if the men *would* shoot one another, but he and Siringo had split up, and Charlie was already moving toward the group.

He had to back the detective's play.

Horn sat his horse and sighted down the barrel of his rifle at the group. They all seemed to be facing down one Mexican, who suddenly put his hand on his gun. Horn wondered if he fired now, would they all started firing at one another?

Siringo moved in closer, keeping close to the steers, gun in hand. He looked around for Clint, saw him not far away, also using the steers for cover.

Now they were both close enough to hear clearly that the argument was over who was in charge. In was obvious that Sandusky was not among them.

Siringo looked over at Clint, who waved that he was ready.

"All right," Siringo announced, stepping out from the cover of the steers, "nobody move."

All the outlaws turned to look at him, and then they all did just the opposite. They went for their guns.

Tom Horn sighted on the Mexican, figuring he was supposed to be the leader. But as the group went for their guns, he could plainly see which one of them was going to clear leather first. He fired, hitting the man in the left side of the neck and putting him down. He quickly levered another round and fired again, this time just into the whole group.

* * *

Siringo fired and ducked back behind the steers, but the animals were just seconds away from stampeding because of the shots.

Clint fired twice, quickly dispatching two men from the action, then took cover himself.

Both men fired into the group of outlaws, who were scattering, trying to make a smaller target of themselves. The steers started to run, but that was of no concern to Siringo and Clint as long as they weren't trampled. They were not worried about keeping the herd together and getting it back to Lincoln County. And, in fact, the herd began to run *toward* the outlaws, who then really had to scramble to keep from being trampled beneath them.

Clint and Siringo managed to avoid that fate themselves, but the stampeding herd kicked up a lot of dust, which impeded their view. They both hoped Horn had a clearer view from above . . .

But he did not.

The dust was obscuring all the figures below him. Horn continued to sight down the barrel of his rifle, though, waiting for a target to become clear. He just hoped Siringo and Clint weren't getting their asses shot off inside the dust cloud.

TWENTY-FIVE

The dust made Siringo's and Clint's eyes gritty, but they had to assume the same was true of the other men. They dodged steers and, finally, to totally avoid being trampled, had to scramble clear of the cover the steers had afforded them.

Several of the outlaws fell prey to the flashing hooves of the stampeding steers. Others scampered out of the way, still trying to see through the clouds of dust to fire at what they assumed were members of a posse. And with no leader to guide them, they simply reacted in an every-man-for-himself manner.

Siringo and Clint worked their way onto the fringes of the dust cloud, were suddenly able to see several outlaws, who were fanning the air in front of them, trying to get a clear view. A shot from Horn's rifle took one down. Clint was hoping they'd capture at least one of them alive.

Eventually, the steers were all gone and the dust began to settle. As the view cleared, the ground was littered with bodies, and there were only a few men standing—Clint, Siringo, and three of the outlaws.

The five men stared at one another, all looking rather shocked by the events of the past few minutes.

"Drop the guns!" Siringo shouted. "It's all over."

The three remaining outlaws had their guns in their hands, pointing down, their faces—like those of Siringo and Clint—covered with dust.

"Don't try anything," Clint said. "You're covered from above."

The three men's eyes flicked about, as if looking for someone to tell them what to do. Finally, one of them began to lift his gun to point it at Clint and Siringo. Horn's rifle barked once and the man fell, startling the other two.

"I told you," Siringo said. "You're covered. Drop your guns."

The two outlaws did not waste any time. They dropped their pistols to the ground.

Siringo looked up at Horn and waved for him to come down.

Clint approached the two men and kicked their guns away, then started checking the fallen.

"All dead," he announced.

The remaining two still seemed shocked.

"Any more?" Siringo asked.

They didn't answer.

"Are there any more of you?" Siringo shouted.

"No, no," one of them said. "Nobody."

"What about Sandusky?" Clint asked.

"Him and Anderson went on ahead," the other said.

"And you fellas agreed to stay behind?" Horn asked. "How stupid can you get?" Horn sat his horse, the stock of his rifle resting on his good thigh so that the barrel was pointed up.

"You fellas were supposed to meet Sandusky somewhere with these cows. You're gonna tell us where that is."

"We can't—"

"Or I'm gonna kill you," Horn added.

The two men looked at Horn's face, realized he was telling the truth, then looked at Siringo.

"It's me or him," Siringo said.

The two men exchanged a glance, then one of them said, "We'll talk."

TWENTY-SIX

"Mexico," one of them said.

"Mexico?" Siringo said. "That's it?"

"That's all we know."

"Well," Clint said, "how were you supposed to find Sandusky?"

"Rosario was supposed to take us there," the second man said. "He knows—knew—his way around Mexico."

"And where's Rosario?" Clint asked.

The man pointed to one of the bodies.

"That's him."

Clint walked over, determined that the man was dead, then went through his pockets.

"He's got nothing," Clint said. "If he knew where to meet Sandusky, he didn't write it down."

"He wouldn't," the first man said.

"Why not?" Siringo asked.

"The Mex didn't know how to read and write."

"You guys are dumber than I thought," Tom Horn said. "I might as well kill you now."

He pointed his rifle at them and they flinched.

"Tom!" Siringo said.

Horn looked at Siringo, then lowered his rifle.

"You're too soft, Charlie," Tom said.

"Maybe they can think of somethin' that will help us," Siringo said.

"Oh yeah? How they gonna do that?"

"We'll take them to the next town and turn them over to the law," Siringo said. He turned to the two outlaws. "If you can come up with somethin' that will help us find Sandusky, it'll work in your favor when you get sentenced. Do you understand?"

"Yeah," one of them said, and then he nudged the other one.

"Yeah, okay."

The outlaw's horse had been driven off by the stampeding cattle. Siringo left Clint and Horn with the two men while he rode down their horses. He would have had Clint help, but he was afraid Horn might kill the two men.

When he brought their horses back, he had the two men mount up, then tied their hands in front of them.

"If you try to ride off," he told them, "I'll let Horn kill you. Understand?"

They both nodded.

"And give it a lot of thought," Siringo said. "The rest of your life depends on it."

Clint had Siringo mounted up, pulled their horses up alongside Clint's.

"There's one more thing," Horn said.

"What's that?" Siringo asked.

"I counted the dead men," Horn said. "There's seven of them."

"And these two makes nine," Clint said. "Anybody else around here?"

"No," Horn said.

"Then we'll be lookin' for three men when we get to Mexico," Siringo said.

"Let's see," Clint said. He rode up to the two prisoners. "Is that right? Are we looking for three more of you? Sandusky and two more men? Anderson?"

The two men exchanged a glance, and then one of them said, "No."

"How many then?" Clint asked.

"You're lookin' for Sandusky and Anderson," the other one said, "and a woman."

"A woman?" Horn asked.

"Delilah," the first outlaw said. "Sandusky's woman."

TWENTY-SEVEN

They rode to the next town, Tularosa, which was only two hours away, so that was all the time the two outlaws had to think. When they got there, they immediately turned the men over to the local sheriff.

Before they left, they visited the two men in their cell.

"What have you got for me?" Siringo asked.

The two men stared at him.

"One of you must've heard somethin'," Siringo said. "Come on!"

"He talked about selling the cattle as soon as we got to Mexico," one of them said.

"So he never intended to drive the cattle deep into Mexico."

"I don't think so."

He looked at the other man.

"I heard Anderson mention Socorro."

"There you go," Siringo said, pointing to him, "that's what I needed."

They left the jailhouse.

* * *

They stopped in a saloon for one beer, and to discuss their options.

"So we goin' to Socorro?" Horn asked.

"El Paso first, I think," Siringo said. "Nobody who rides near El Paso doesn't go there. It's an easy crossin' into Mexico."

They both looked at Clint.

"What do you think?"

"I don't think Sandusky ever expected these men to get to Mexico with the cattle," he said. "I think he left them to get caught or killed, and to give them time to get to Mexico, where they figure a posse can't go."

"They're right," Siringo said. "A posse can't go to Mexico. But we can."

"So he never wanted the cattle," Horn said.

"I think he figured if the men actually got the cattle to Mexico, then he'd sell them and that would be extra. But he wasn't counting on it."

"So what do we think?" Siringo asked. "El Paso?"

"El Paso," Horn said.

"El Paso," Clint said.

They headed for El Paso.

TWENTY-EIGHT

El Paso, Texas, was where Texas, New Mexico, and Mexico came together. El Paso and Juarez, Mexico, were joined together by a bridge, and were pretty much considered to be one city.

With the arrival of the railroads in 1881, the population boomed, but that included everyone from merchants and businessmen and priests, to gunfighters and prostitutes. El Paso became violent and wild, well known for its prostitution and gambling. No traveler in his right mind would bypass it. Siringo, Clint, and Horn were hopeful that Harlan Sandusky would not be able to resist it either.

As they rode in, Horn said, "Jesus, I ain't been here in a while. What a change."

"The railroad has brought everything in here," Siringo said, "good and bad."

"We need to get a hotel," Clint said. "We might as well get some rest while we're here, and find out if Sandusky is either here, or just passed through."

"Agreed," Siringo said.

Horn didn't say a word, but he had to be happy about having a chance to rest.

They dropped Horn off in front of a hotel to have him get them three rooms, and then Clint and Siringo took the horses to the livery. When they returned to the hotel, they only had to collect their keys from the clerk.

"Tom can use this time to rest," Siringo said as they walked up the stairs.

"It'll do him some good," Clint said. "Also a couple of good, hot meals while we're here."

"When was the last time you were here?" Siringo asked.

"Back when Dallas Stoudemire was the law," Clint said. "He was killed soon after."

"That's a while."

"Yeah," Clint said, "it's been built up."

"Why don't we just drop our gear in our rooms and then go and talk to the local law?"

"Sure," Clint said. "Let's stop in on Tom and tell him we'll pick him up when it's time to eat."

"Okay."

They went to their respective rooms, dropped off their rifles and saddlebags, then walked to Horn's room, the number of which the clerk had given them.

"Come on in!" Horn called when they knocked.

As they entered, they saw him sitting up on the bed with his gun next to him.

"We're gonna go talk to the sheriff," Siringo said.

"I'll come along." Horn started to get off the bed.

"Why don't you stay here and give that leg some rest?" Clint suggested. "We'll come and get you when we're ready to eat."

Horn sat back and said, "I could use a hot meal and a cold beer."

"We could all use that," Siringo said. "We won't be long."

"Watch your backs," Horn said.

"Right," Siringo said, and they left.

The sheriff's office was not where it had been when Clint was last in El Paso. A new one had been built a couple of blocks away. The wood used to build it still looked new, although the new wood smell had faded. The shingle outside had not faded, however. It said: SHERIFF EDWARD JENKINS.

They knocked, and entered.

The first thing Clint noticed was that the inside was clean. Not usually something you noticed about a sheriff's office.

There was a small desk set against a wall, so that the man seated at it was sitting sideways to the door. He turned his head to see who had entered, then turned his body so they could see the star on his chest.

"Help you fellas?" he asked. He was in his late thirties, clean shaven and as neat as the office looked. There was even a shine on the badge.

"Sheriff," Siringo said, "my name is Charlie Siringo. I work for the Pinkerton Agency."

"Mr. Siringo," the lawman said, standing up, "I assume you have bona fides?"

"Yes, sir."

Siringo produced his credentials, which the sheriff looked over very carefully.

"And you, sir?"

"My name's Clint Adams."

"I assume you can prove that?"

"Well, I'm not a Pinkerton, so I have no credentials," Clint said. "I guess you'll just have to take my word for it."

The sheriff didn't act like he'd ever heard Clint's name before. He simply turned his attention to Siringo.

"What can I do for you?"

"We're trackin' a man named Harlan Sandusky," Siringo said, "did some rustlin' and killed some people in New Mexico."

"Don't know him."

"Well, we have reason to believe he either passed through here, or he's here now."

Sheriff Jenkins shook his head and said, "Not that I know of."

"Do you see all strangers who come to town?" Clint asked.

"More or less," Jenkins said.

"Have you got deputies?" Siringo asked.

"Two," the man said, nodding.

"You mind if we ask them?"

"Not at all," Jenkins said. "Billy's out there now, making rounds. Walt will be in later."

"Billy and Walt," Siringo said. "Thanks, Sheriff."

As they turned to leave, the lawman said, "Whoa, hold on."

They stopped and looked at him.

"Neither one of you is wearing a badge," Jenkins said, "so I'm not going to want any gunplay in my town." He seemed to be looking at Clint when he said that, which led Clint to believe the lawman had recognized his name.

"Believe me, Sheriff," Siringo said, "if we can take Sandusky and his men without firing a shot, we will. But if it comes to that . . ."

"If either one of you kills a man in El Paso," Jenkins said, "you'll have to answer to me. I will not tolerate it."

He came across more like a stern schoolteacher than a sheriff.

"Well, Sheriff," Siringo said, "we'll sure keep that in mind."

TWENTY-NINE

Clint and Siringo went back to the hotel to collect Horn. Between the sheriff's office and the hotel they had passed a steakhouse, so they retraced their steps and stopped there.

"Away from the window," Siringo said when the waiter tried to seat them in front.

"Of course, sir," the waiter said, and took them to a table against the back wall, as far from the window as they could get.

"We'll take three steak dinners, fast as you can," Siringo said.

"Yes, sir."

"And three cold beers," Clint said.

"Comin' up."

Horn shifted in his seat, trying to get comfortable.

"Okay," he said finally, "what happened with the local law?"

"I think he used to be a schoolteacher," Siringo said. "He was very stern with us, wanted us to know how much he'd take offense if we killed anyone in his town."

"You tell him about me?"

"No."

"Good. What about Sandusky?"

"Claims he never heard of him," Clint said. "He's got two deputies, though. Maybe one of them actually knows what he's doing."

"We'll find 'em after we eat," Siringo said, "and ask 'em."

The waiter brought the three beers, promised that their meals would be out in a minute.

"We don't find Sandusky here, we'll have to check across the bridge," Siringo said.

"And failing that," Clint said, "all of Mexico."

"I been to Mexico before," Horn said.

"We all have," Siringo said. "Maybe we'll get lucky and Sandusky hasn't been to Mexico and doesn't know his way around."

"We can catch up to him while he's stumbling around," Horn said.

"He's got Anderson with him," Clint said. "His *segundo*. And his woman. One of them is bound to have been to Mexico before."

"You're probably right," Siringo said.

"Maybe we'll get lucky and he's still here, or across the bridge," Horn said.

"Why don't we split up?" Siringo offered. "We can cover more ground that way. I'll go across the bridge and check in Juarez. You two stay here and check around."

"And if you find them, you won't try to take them alone?" Clint asked.

"Of course not," Siringo said.

"I've got a better idea," Clint said. "You two started this thing together. I'll go to Juarez and you two check here. That way if you find them, you'll be two against two."

"You're sayin' you'd be able to handle the two of them better than I would?" Siringo asked.

Clint stared at Siringo and said, "I'll let you answer that."

Before Siringo could answer, the waiter arrived with their steak dinners, set down the steaming plates, and asked, "Anythin' else?"

"Not right now," Clint said.

The waiter nodded and left.

Clint picked up his knife and fork and looked at Siringo.

"So?"

"Yeah, yeah, okay," Siringo said. "You're right. You'd have a better chance against the two of them than I would."

Horn laughed, cut into his meat, and said, "I coulda tol' ya that."

THIRTY

After they finished eating, they firmed up their plans.

"I'll go right from here to Juarez," Clint said.

"And Tom and I will look for Sandusky, and look for those deputies, see if they know anything."

"We know what Sandusky looks like," Horn said. "You don't. Maybe I should go with you."

"Just describe him," Clint said. "That should do it."

Horn left it to Siringo to give Clint a solid description of the outlaw.

"Okay," Clint said. "I've got it."

"I assume you've been to Juarez before," Siringo said.

"Many times."

"Good," the detective said. "Well, let's get this going. If he's here, I want to put our hands on him tonight."

They stood up, paid their bill, and walked out onto the street. There they split, agreeing to meet at the hotel in three hours, whether they found something or not.

* * *

Clint crossed the bridge into Juarez, which was the larger populated of the two-in-one town of El Paso and Juarez. The majority of the populace was Mexican, and Clint, a gringo, drew looks as he walked the streets.

He thought about visiting the sheriff of Juarez, but it was a fact that most of the lawmen in Mexico were crooked—or at least out for their own interests. But there was one person in any town who could answer most questions, and that was the bartender.

Clint walked through Juarez until he found a large cantina with music, girls, food, and drink. A man liked Harlan Sandusky would not be able to resist such a place.

He entered, ignored the looks that came his way, and walked to the bar. Several Mexicans turned to look at him . . .

Then move away to allow him some space. At the end of the bar a few men had their heads together, and then the word started to spread through the place.

Somebody had recognized him, and within a few minutes the entire place knew the Gunsmith was there.

"Cerveza," he told the bartender.

In El Paso, Siringo and Horn walked the streets, keeping a wary eye out for Sandusky or Anderson.

Siringo walked at Horn's pace, which was steady while not being brisk.

They stopped whenever they came to a saloon, and there was no shortage of saloons in El Paso.

They were standing at the bar in one saloon, holding beers, when Siringo said, "We're not gonna be able to have a drink every time we stop in a saloon."

"Agreed," Horn said. "We know you can't hold your liquor, Charlie."

"I was thinkin' of you, Horn," Siringo said.

"Don't worry about me," Horn said. "I'm fine."

Siringo looked into Horn's eyes, which were red-rimmed. He just didn't know if it was from drinking, from being tired, or from pain. Maybe all three. Or maybe the drinking was dulling the pain.

"In fact," Horn said, "I'm thinkin' maybe we should split up."

"I don't think that's a good idea, Tom," Siringo said. "We're lookin' for two men, but we don't know how many more they may have recruited since they got here."

Horn sipped his beer and said, "Yeah, you're probably right. I'm just gettin' impatient."

At that point the batwing doors opened and a man stepped in. He looked around the room, but it was only when he turned to approach the bar that they saw his deputy's badge.

As he walked to the bar, they could see he was about Horn's age.

"Hey, Johnny," he yelled to the bartender, "gimme a short one."

"The sheriff don't like you drinkin' on duty, Billy," the bartender pointed out.

"Well, the sheriff ain't here," Billy said, "and why do you think I asked for a short one?"

The bartender shook his head, drew a short beer for the deputy, and set it on the bar.

"Thanks."

"Put that on my tab, bartender," Siringo said.

The deputy looked at Siringo and said, "Thanks, mister."

"Don't mention it," Siringo said. "But I'm gonna ask for somethin' in return."

The deputy sipped his beer, eyed both Siringo and Horn, then asked, "Oh? What's that?"

"Just some information," Siringo said. "See, we talked to the sheriff earlier, and he said you might be able to help us."

"Yeah? How do I know you talked to the sheriff?"

"Sheriff Jenkins said he had two deputies, Billy and Walt," Siringo said.

"Yeah, that's right. And who are you?"

"I'm Charlie Siringo," the detective said. "This is Tom Horn."

"Hey," Billy said, "hey, I hearda both of you."

"Will you help us?" Siringo asked.

"I will if I can," Billy said.

"We're looking for two men and a woman," Siringo said. "One of the men is very big, the other kinda slender but tall."

"And the woman?"

"Not pretty," Siringo said, "dressed like a man, wearin' a gun like one."

"Huh," Billy said, "I gotta admit I only notice pretty women, but I ain't seen nobody like the three of them. Not around here."

"What about your partner?" Horn asked.

"Partner?"

"Walt," Siringo said.

"Oh, Walt," Billy said. "He ain't my partner, just the other deputy."

"Okay, where is he?"

"He'll be on duty in a few hours," Billy said. "But he won't know nothin'."

"Why not?"

"Because he's useless," Billy said, "old and useless. That's why the sheriff makes him work at night, when nothin's goin' on."

"Well," Siringo said, "we can ask him anyway."

"Suit yourself," Billy said. He finished his beer. "I gotta keep doin' my rounds. See you."

Billy walked out.

"Talk about useless," Siringo said.

"Didn't ask us any questions," Horn said. "Not much of a deputy himself."

"Don't matter," Siringo said. "We won't need anythin' else from him."

Horn put his empty mug down.

"So I guess we better keep lookin'," Horn said.

THIRTY-ONE

Sandusky looked at the women on the bed.

The Mexican whore was slender, with small breasts and long, black hair. Her skin was dark, and she smelled like *frijoles*.

On the other hand, Delilah was full-bodied—not fat, but meaty—with big breasts, red hair, and she smelled like . . . well, sex. Sweat, dirt, but sex, too.

They hadn't had time to take a bath, so they had just picked out a whore and gone to her room with her. Sandusky had both women undress for him. The Mexican's nipples were dark brown, Delilah's light brown. The whore's were small, Delilah's large.

"It is your turn to undress, *señor*," the girl said. "You look like a big *gringo* to me."

"Oh, he is," Delilah said. "Very big." She reached out and touched one of the whore's breasts. She rubbed the smooth skin, touched the nipple with her fingertips.

"Don't start without me, ladies," Sandusky said.

He took off his shirt, revealing a torso like a slab of rocks. Next he pulled off his boots and socks, then his britches. His cock was erect, throbbing, and red. The whore's eyes went wide.

"Señor," she said. *"Muy grande."*

"Yes, he is," Delilah said, pinching the whore's nipple.

Clint sipped his beer and looked around the noisy cantina. He was the center of attention. That was okay. Most of them just wanted to look. But there were others who wanted to do more than look. He could tell because he knew the expression on their faces, and in their eyes. It was hunger. A hunger for fame, and reputation.

If they'd only ask him, he could tell them that neither was what they were all cracked up to be.

There were five of them, and they all stood up from their table.

He put his beer on the bar.

José Rios recognized the Gunsmith as soon as he walked in. He passed the word, which flowed through the room like wildfire. It eventually reached the table where Rodrigo Fuentes and his men were sitting.

"Can it really be him?" one of them asked.

"There is one way to find out, Carlos," Fuentes said. "Are we ready, *amigos*?"

"We have always been ready, Rodrigo," Bernardo said.

"Will others join us?" Eduardo asked.

"Only one way to find that out, too, *es verdad*?" Fuentes asked.

Yes, it was true.

They stood up.

* * *

Clint watched the five men stand up, with steely resolve on all their faces. Usually, in a group like that, he could count on one or two who were acting out of fear, or against their will. Not this time. Every one of these men knew what they were up against and they were ready—even anxious—for it.

And it was infectious.

As they stood, several others also stepped forward. Those who were not involved quickly moved away. It was as if the population of the cantina was suddenly drawn to the walls.

Leaving a big circle in the center.

When the word reached one man in the back of the room, he wasn't sure it was true. But he heard the buzz moving through the room. He waited, and when suddenly the center of the room was cleared out, he could see what was happening.

One man standing at the bar alone.

At least nine others, facing him, all armed with pistols.

He shook his head.

His goal had been to remain unnoticed in this cantina, unidentified for as long as he could. But he could not stand aside and watch this.

Not when he knew that the lone man was Clint Adams, the Gunsmith.

His friend.

He took his badge from his pocket, pinned it on, and then stood up.

"Attencion!" he shouted.

All eyes went to him.

"I am a federal marshal from New Mexico," he said. "This will not happen."

Rodrigo Fuentes looked at the young man with the badge and frowned.

"You are foolish," he said. "This will happen, and you cannot stop it."

"You misunderstand me, *señor*," the lawman said. "What I meant to say was, this will not happen . . . without me."

Clint looked at the man with the badge, shook his head, and smiled. He hadn't seen the young man in some time, and was not surprised to find him standing behind a badge.

"Hello, Baca," he said.

"Hello, Clint."

Fuentes looked at the man with the badge and said, "You are even more foolish than I thought. This is not your business."

"I am making it my business."

"Very well," Fuentes said, "if we are to kill you as well, we should know your name."

"Gladly," the man said. "My name is Baca, Elfego Baca."

THIRTY-TWO

Sandusky approached the bed.

Delilah seemed to be entranced by the Mexican whore's delicate breast and nipple. While she stroked the right one, Sandusky reached out to touch the left. The whore closed her eyes and got a dreamy look on her lips as the gringo and gringa played with her. Her name was Juanita, and unlike the forty-year-old Delilah, she was very young, and very pretty.

Abruptly, Sandusky put his hand over her face and pushed her onto her back. She opened her eyes in surprise, gasped as he grabbed her by the ankles and spread her. It was his favorite way to take a woman, although later he planned to have her on all fours as well.

Delilah knew the whore was going to come out of this battered and bruised, and she smiled, because better Juanita than her.

Sandusky pressed the head of his penis against the whore's pussy and then shoved. The woman gasped, but the cry was muffled when Delilah pressed her mouth to the whore's lips and stuck her tongue in her mouth . . .

* * *

Baca moved across the room to stand next to Clint Adams. He was twenty-three years old and looked younger, but he commanded attention. He was best known for the "Miracle of the Jacal," where he stood off a host of gunmen from inside a small building which was eventually decimated by gunfire—and came out without a scratch. And that was before he ever started wearing a badge.

"Nice to see you," Clint said.

"Later you can tell me what you are doing here," Baca said, "other than looking for trouble."

"You know me," Clint said, "I never go looking for trouble."

They turned to face the nine men across the room from them.

"Señores," Rodrigo Fuentes said, "it is our honor to be the men who kill *Señores* Clint Adams and Elfego Baca."

"Jesus Christ," Clint muttered to Baca, "is he thanking us?"

"My people are nothin' if not polite, *señor*," Baca said. "Unlike most gringos I have met."

Siringo and Horn came out of another saloon and ran smack into three men who were about to go in.

"Well, well," one of the men said, "look who's here. What a coincidence."

"Excuse me—" Siringo started before he realized they were looking at the three Monroe brothers.

"Hello, Horn," Josh Monroe said, "remember me and my brothers, Dal and Ed?"

"I remember," Horn said. "Now get out of the way."

"Not so fast," Josh said. "We got unfinished business."

Siringo was busy wondering how the Monroe brothers

had caught up with them. They were fairly certain they had not been tailed by anyone, yet here they were. A coincidence? He hated those as much as Clint did.

"Look," Horn said, "we're kinda busy now. Why don't you see me tomorrow?"

"Tomorrow?" Josh asked. "Out here on the street?"

"Sure," Horn said, "you'd much rather get killed in daylight, wouldn't you?"

"And where's your friend, the Gunsmith?" Josh asked. "You sure you can handle the three of us without him to back your play?"

"I don't think we'll have a problem," Horn said. "Now excuse us."

Horn and Siringo walked around the three men and crossed the street to the other side.

"You just agreed that we," Siringo said, stressing the "we," "are gonna meet them in the street tomorrow."

"So what?" Horn asked. "We can handle them, even without Clint."

"Are you sure?"

"Positive," Horn said. "None if those brothers are gun-hands."

"And we got the sheriff watchin' us close to make sure we don't kill anybody in his town," Siringo pointed out.

"I didn't promise," Horn said. "You can stand aside if you like. I think I can take 'em."

"Yeah, well, I can't afford to have you killed by three idiot brothers until after we find Sandusky," Siringo said, "so I think I'll just tag along."

"Suit yourself," Horn said. "Let's hit another saloon."

"Let's see if we can find that other deputy," Siringo said, "Walt."

THIRTY-THREE

Clint and Baca stood fast in front of the bar, watching. Neither of them knew these men, but they knew who the leader was, so they were going to have to keep an eye on him. When he moved, everybody would move.

Rodrigo Fuentes went for his gun.

Sandusky was wearing the whore out when he heard the shots. Delilah pulled her big tit from the whore's mouth and looked around nervously.

"What the hell—" Sandusky said.

In minutes the shooting stopped, and there was a banging on the door.

"What the hell—" Sandusky said again, grabbing his gun.

Both Clint and Baca cleanly outdrew all nine men. They fired quickly, Clint fanning his gun.

Later many men would say they were there when the Gunsmith and Elfego Baca gunned down twenty men without ever moving from where they stood. That would, of course, be a slight exaggeration, and not as legendary a story as Baca's jacal tale.

Between them they had twelve bullets for nine men, and they made them all count.

All nine men were on the floor dead in seconds.

"Madre de Dios," someone said.

They quickly ejected their empty shells and reloaded, then walked among the bodies to be sure they were dead. They were.

"There should be a lawman here soon," Baca said.

"You think so?" Clint asked.

"We had better have a drink, *amigo*," Baca said. He looked at the bartender. *"Dos cervezas."*

"Sí, señor," the bartender said, acting quickly.

Surprisingly, no one had left the cantina. They were still quiet, though, staring down at the bodies of the dead men.

"Well," Clint said, "we've got plenty of witnesses here."

"I am sure we will have no problems," Marshal Baca said.

"Something tells me you know the local lawman."

Baca smiled.

"I did stop in to see him when I first arrived," the younger man admitted.

"When was that?" Clint asked. "And why?"

"I arrived several days ago," Baca said. "I am looking for a man named Steagall."

"What'd he do?"

"Murder," Baca said. "I was trying to remain unknown, waiting for him to walk in."

"Sorry to ruin it for you," Clint said. "You may have been able to get him today."

"Quien sabe," Baca said. "We will see. There is still time. Why are you here?"

"I'm riding with Charlie Siringo and Tom Horn," Clint said.

"I have heard of them, but not met them," Baca said.

"We're trailing a man named Harlan Sandusky and his gang."

"For what offense?"

"Rustling, probably murder."

"How many do you seek?"

"Two men and a woman."

Baca rubbed his nose.

"When did they arrive?"

"No way of telling, but maybe the past couple of days. We're hoping he's still here."

Baca drank his beer and set the mug down heavily.

"Clint, I believe you are in luck!"

Sandusky swung the door open and pointed his gun at the man in the hall.

"Hey, take it easy!" Anderson said.

"What's goin' on?"

"We gotta get outta here. There's been a shootout in the cantina."

"Siringo?"

"No," Anderson said. "The Gunsmith, and Elfego Baca. And Baca's wearin' a badge."

Sandusky frowned. "They may not be here for us, but we better get out of here anyway."

He turned and looked at Delilah. She was still sniffing around the whore, getting dangerously close to the girl's pussy.

"Delilah!" he snapped. "Get yer clothes on or I'll leave ya here!"

"All right!" Delilah gave one of the girl's nipples a quick lick and then reached for her clothes.

THIRTY-FOUR

"Here?" Clint asked.

"In the back," Baca said. "They went back with one of the whores."

"All of them?"

"All three," Baca said. "The woman is not attractive, but there is something . . . earthy about her. And I just happen to like older women."

"Show me where they went."

"I will do better than that," Baca said. "I will back your play."

They looked around. The crowd was now milling about the dead men, maybe even lifting some of their belongings. A lawman still had not arrived.

"We better get this done, *amigo*, before the law arrives," Baca said. "This way."

Baca led Clint through the crowd to a curtained doorway in the back. Beyond that was a long hallway, with doors on either side.

They found one door unlocked, opened it, and discovered

it empty, moved on to the next one. In there they found a woman, in her thirties, sitting half dressed on her bed.

"A man and a woman, were they here?" Clint asked.

"No," she said, "only one man. The man and woman. They were next door with Juanita."

"Thanks."

They moved on to the next door, opened it, and found a naked woman—a girl, really—on a bed.

"Where are they?" Clint asked.

"Who?" the girl asked.

"The man and the woman who were with you," Clint said.

Baca said something to the girl in Spanish.

"What'd you tell her?"

"That if she didn't answer, I'd arrest her," Baca said. "Ask her again."

"Where are they?"

"They left when they heard the shooting," she said.

"Which way?"

"The back."

"Do me a favor," Clint said to Baca. "Stay with her so she doesn't disappear. She still might know something useful."

"I will find out," Baca said. "Go."

Clint nodded, left the room, and went down the hall to the back. He found a back door, went out, and found himself behind the cantina. He looked both ways, didn't see anyone or hear anything. He wondered if they had fled on foot, or if they'd had their horses tied up there. The ground was too hard for him to be able to tell, but Horn might be able to read it.

He went back inside.

* * *

Siringo and Horn found Walt, the deputy, in a small saloon, and immediately saw what Billy had been talking about. He was a shrunken man in his sixties with a face full of wrinkles. He had one hand wrapped around a glass of whiskey. Maybe they'd gotten to him, though, before he could get too drunk.

"Are you Walt?" Siringo asked.

"That's me," the little man answered proudly. "Walt the deputy."

Apparently, he'd already had a few drinks.

"My name's Charlie Siringo," Siringo said. "I'm a Pinkerton."

"Hey, congratulations," Walt said. "Let's have a drink on that."

"Later," Siringo said, putting his hand on the man's arm to keep him from drinking. "The sheriff said I could ask you some questions. He also said you were the man to help me."

"He said that?" Walt stood straighter. "He really said that?"

"Yeah, he did."

"Well then, go ahead and ask," Walt said. "I'll help ya if I can."

"We're lookin' for three people, two men and a woman."

"A pretty woman?" Walt asked.

"No, not a pretty woman," Siringo said, "but from what we hear, she ain't ugly. But she dresses like a man and wears a gun."

Walt looked surprised.

"I saw a woman like that!" he said excitedly.

"Where?"

"On the street."

"When?" Horn asked.

Walt looked at Horn as if just realizing he was there.

"Is he with you?" he asked Siringo.

"He is," Siringo said. "Answer his question, please."

"What was the question?" Walt asked, squinting as if it would help him hear better.

"When did you see her?" Horn asked.

"Um, musta been a couple of days ago."

"Where?" Siringo asked again.

"On the street."

"Yeah, but where? What street?"

Walt frowned, then said, "I dunno. Somewhere."

"Was she with anybody?" Siringo asked.

"No, she was by herself," Walt said.

"What did she look like?" Horn asked.

"Like you said," Walt answered, "not pretty, but she had what a man likes." Walt put his hands up in front of his chest.

"We understand," Siringo said.

"Are you sure you can't tell us what street you saw her on?" Horn asked.

"This town's got a lot of streets," Walt said.

Siringo and Horn exchanged a frustrated glance. The detective released Walt's arm so he could drink, then said to the bartender, "Give him another drink."

"Thanks, Pinkerton!" Walt said.

"Yeah, you're welcome."

"Drink with me?" Walt asked.

"Next time," Siringo said.

He and Horn turned and headed for the door.

"Hey, Pinkertons!" Walt yelled.

They both turned.

"The bridge."

"What about the bridge?" Siringo asked.

"That's where I saw the woman," Walt said. "Goin' over the bridge."

"To Juarez?" Horn said.

"Yup," Walt said. "The bridge." He waved an arm. "Over."

"Have you seen her since then?" Siringo asked.

"Nope," Walt said, "only that one time."

"How do you remember that?" Horn asked.

"Hey," Walt said, "I may be old, but I ain't dead, ya know?"

"Yeah," Siringo said. "Okay, thanks."

They went out the door, stopped on the boardwalk right outside.

"If she went to Juarez," Horn said, "maybe the three of them are there."

"And Clint's gonna run into them."

"We gotta get over there," Horn said. "It's dark, there's no tellin' what could happen."

"Yeah," Siringo said, "let's go."

THIRTY-FIVE

Clint came back to the room and found Baca kneeling in front of the woman. As he entered, the young marshal stood up.

"Find anything?" Baca asked.

"No," Clint said. "They're gone. I'll need Tom Horn to see if he can find any sign. How about her?"

"She says she was afraid of them," Baca said. "The man was brutal, the woman was . . . well, Juanita says she likes men, but the woman was all over her . . . touching her . . . she didn't like it, but they were paying her."

"Did she hear them say anything about where they were going from here?" Clint asked. "Socorro, maybe?"

"No, nothing," Baca said. "They didn't talk in front of her."

Somebody showed up in the doorway and both men turned and looked. Clint saw a man with a sombrero and a sheriff's star.

"Que pasa?" the sheriff said. "What the hell is going on, Elfego?"

"Antonio," Baca said, "let us go to your office so we can talk."

"Sandusky?" the sheriff asked.

"That's the name," Clint said.

"I do not know him."

"Well," Clint said, "I'm riding with Charlie Siringo and Tom Horn to find him."

"And you think he is here?"

"I know he is," Clint said. "That girl Juanita told us so."

"She told you his name?" the sheriff asked. "The name of the man and woman she was with?"

"No, but—"

"And you?" the sheriff said. "You are still looking for . . . what was his name?"

"Steagall."

"*Sí*, Steagall. And you just happened to be in that cantina tonight?"

"That is right."

The lawman stared at the two of them.

"The two of you killed nine men tonight," he said. "What am I supposed to do about that?"

"Talk to the witnesses," Baca said. "You will see we had no choice."

"You could have minded your own business," the sheriff said to Baca.

"And Clint would be dead," Baca said. "Would you like Juarez to be known as the place where the Gunsmith was killed?"

"All right, fine," the lawman said. "Get out."

"You have not talked to the witnesses yet?" Baca said.

"Yes, I have," the sheriff said. "When are you leaving town?"

"Not 'til I catch Steagall," Baca said.

"I'm leaving tomorrow," Clint said. "Actually, I'm going back over the bridge tonight."

"Bueno," the lawman said. "That is good. Now go."

Clint and Baca left the office.

"Elfego, I wish I could stay and help you with your problem," Clint said. "I owe you my life tonight."

"We are far from even, my friend," Baca said. "Besides, I do not need help. My man is alone. Yours is not."

The two men shook hands. "I didn't even buy you a drink," Clint said.

"Next time, my friend," Baca said. "Next time."

THIRTY-SIX

Clint was halfway across the bridge to El Paso when he saw Siringo and Horn coming toward him.

"They're in Juarez," Siringo said. "We found out one of the deputies saw the girl crossing the bridge."

"I know," Clint said. "I found them."

"You did?" Siringo asked.

"And lost them."

"You did?" Horn asked.

"Where?" Siringo asked.

"In a cantina," Clint said. "They were in a back room with a whore."

"All of them?" Siringo asked.

"Well, Sandusky and the woman."

"You didn't see them?" Horn asked.

"No," Clint said, "there was some trouble, and they ran out the back and disappeared."

"On foot, or horseback?" Horn asked.

"I don't know," Clint said. "I couldn't tell."

"Well, take us there," Horn said. "Maybe I can tell."

* * *

Clint took Siringo and Horn to the back of the cantina. He and the detective stood aside while Horn studied the ground. He finished telling Siringo everything that had happened.

"Elfego Baca, huh?" Siringo said. "That was a lucky coincidence."

Clint made a face at that word, but in this case it had worked in his favor.

"And the girl they were with didn't know anythin'?" Siringo asked.

"Apparently not," Clint said. "She was just upset because the woman with Sandusky was touching her."

"Maybe I should talk to her," Siringo said. "I might ask her something you didn't."

"Wait a minute," Clint said, you speak Spanish, right?"

"I do."

"Baca was translating for me," Clint said. "Maybe something got lost in the translation."

Clint tried the back door, found it still open.

"Tom," Siringo said, "we're goin' inside for a minute."

Horn waved at them to go.

Inside Clint found his way to the girl's room again, and they tried the door. It was locked. They pressed their ears to the door.

"Somebody's in there," Clint said.

"What the hell," Siringo said, and knocked.

He had to knock a second time before the girl answered. She opened the door about six inches and said, "I am busy."

"Remember me, Juanita?"

She looked at him, then at Siringo, who said something to her in Spanish. She answered him.

"We can talk right here," Siringo said to Clint. "We don't have to go in."

"Okay," Clint said.

Siringo and the girl began to talk rapidly. Clint wasn't catching much of it beyond *hombre* and *mujer*, "man" and "woman." For a moment he saw movement inside, a man's bare leg, but that was it. The girl hadn't wasted any time going back to work.

Suddenly, Clint heard the girl say the word "Socorro."

"What'd she say?"

"Apparently," Siringo said, "the man and woman she was with didn't think she could speak much English, or understand. And, in fact, she can't. But she did hear one of them say 'Socorro.' " She said something to Siringo. "The woman. Then the man snapped at her."

"Probably told her to shut up."

"Socorro," Clint said. "That's what we figured."

"Let's let the girl go back to work," Siringo suggested.

"Sure."

Siringo said something to her, then she said, *"Gracias,"* and closed the door.

They went back out to the alley, where Horn was waiting.

"No horses," he said. "They were on foot, probably went that way." He pointed. "They're probably goin' to pick up their horses."

"We could check livery stables all over Juarez and see where they were," Siringo said.

"Or," Clint said, "we could mount up in the morning and head for Socorro."

"Socorro came up?" Horn asked.

"The whore heard the woman say it," Siringo said.

"Well then, that's my vote," Horn said. "To hell with

Juarez—which, by the way, stinks to high heaven—and El Paso."

"Okay, then," Siringo said, "we might as well head back over the bridge and get some sleep. In the morning we'll make for Socorro."

They were all agreed.

THIRTY-SEVEN

The next morning Sandusky, Anderson, and Delilah rode into Socorro.

"Boss," Anderson said, "shouldn't we keep goin'? Further into Mexico? The men aren't gonna get here with the cattle."

"We'll keep goin'," Sandusky said, "but not further into Mexico. We're gonna double back into the States."

"But . . . we don't even know who's after us," Anderson said. "If we got the Gunsmith and Elfego Baca after us—"

"They'll never expect us to double back," Sandusky said.

"So when do we do that?"

"After we meet the rest of the men."

"The rest—"

"I sent some telegrams, Cal," Sandusky said. "We've got a new crew waitin' for us here. And if the Gunsmith and Baca or anybody else want to catch up to us here, we'll take care of them."

"How many men?"

"I'm not sure," Sandusky said. "Let's go and find out."

*   *   *

Socorro was an easy ride from El Paso, but when Clint walked the horses from the livery to the hotel, he saw the problem immediately. The Monroe brothers were standing across the street.

He went inside, found Siringo and Horn in the lobby.

"How'd the Monroe brothers get here?" he asked.

"Oh, that," Horn said. "Yeah, we saw them last night."

"Must be a coincidence."

"Yeah, some coincidence," Siringo said. "Horn told them he—we—would meet them in the street today."

"And me?" Clint asked.

"They don't know you're here," Horn said.

"Well," Clint said, "they know now."

"Maybe that'll change their minds," Siringo said hopefully. "I really don't want to kill anybody today—not unless I have to."

"We backed them down once," Horn commented. "Maybe we can do it again."

The three of them went outside. As they stepped into the street, so did the three Monroe brothers.

"Looks like they're determined," Siringo said.

"Horn!" Josh Monroe called. "It's time, and even havin' the Gunsmith with ya ain't gonna change our minds."

"That's too bad," Horn called back, "but come ahead. Let's get this over with. We have to ride out."

"This is for our brother," John said.

The three of them went for their guns. Clint, Siringo, and Horn drew calmly and they each shot a Monroe Brother dead.

As they reloaded and holstered their weapons, Clint said, "I'd still like to know how they got here."

"Let's get out of here before the sheriff tries to keep us from leavin'," Siringo said. "We need to get to Socorro."

They mounted up and rode out, leaving the three dead men in the street.

Sandusky led Anderson and Delilah to a small cantina and dismounted.

"They should be inside," Sandusky said, "if they're not off someplace with a whore or two."

"Do I know these fellas?" Anderson asked.

"You'll know some of them," Sandusky said. "I know most of them. Others I hired because of their reps."

They tied off their horses and went inside. Several men looked up from their table.

"Hey, Harlan," one of them yelled.

"Hey, Kane."

The two men shook hands, and Kane waved an arm.

"Meet your new gang."

"You know Cal Anderson, right?" Sandusky asked.

"Sure," Kane said. He gave a nod to Cal, who returned it.

"And who's this?" Kane asked. He was a big, bald man with long arms that were corded with muscle.

"That's Delilah," Sandusky said. "She's mine."

Kane put his hands up and said, "Okay."

Sandusky looked around. There were six men in the place. He had been hoping for a dozen.

"Where are the Monroe brothers?" he asked.

"In El Paso," one of the other men said. His name was Hill. "Said they had some business with Tom Horn."

"Horn is in El Paso?" Sandusky asked.

"According to the Monroe brothers," Hill said.

Sandusky frowned. Horn was supposed to be dead. So

was Siringo. But if they were alive, they—and the Gunsmith *and* Elfego Baca—could be a problem.

"Anybody know anythin' about Elfego Baca?" he asked.

A Mexican named Francisco said, "He's wearing a marshal's badge, lookin' for a man named Steagall."

"I know Steagall," Sandusky said. "If Baca's trackin' him, then he ain't after us."

"That leaves Horn," Anderson said, "and the Gunsmith, and maybe Siringo."

"Yeah," Sandusky said. He looked around again. "Anybody missin' besides the Monroes?"

"Mackie and Lewis are in the back with a whore," Kane said. "They only got one, so we gotta share her."

So that made eight men—nine with Kane. The Monroes had probably gone and gotten themselves killed. Add himself, Anderson, and Delilah, that made twelve. Against two, maybe three.

"Okay," Sandusky said, "from this point on, everybody stays sober. We're probably gonna have to use our guns today."

"On who?" Kane asked.

"Let's get a beer and I'll tell you."

"I thought you said we had to stay sober."

"Yeah, sober," Sandusky said. "I didn't say we had to stay dry."

THIRTY-EIGHT

Eventually, all the men were in the cantina. Some of them were eyeing Delilah, obviously preferring her to the local whore. She stayed right next to Sandusky.

Sandusky reinforced his decision about drinking.

"The first man I see drunk gets fired," he said. "If you can't handle your liquor, then don't drink."

"When are these men supposed to be comin' here?" Kane asked.

"They should be here today," Sandusky said. "I'll want you men placed strategically around the town."

"How many are we sure of?"

"Seems like Horn and Clint Adams are for sure," Sandusky said. "Charlie Siringo might be with them, if he's not dead."

"We got a big advantage, "Kane said.

"What about the Gunsmith?" Hill asked. "Even with the amount of men we have, I ain't lookin' to go up against him."

"We ain't gonna go up against him," Sandusky said.

"We're gonna ambush him. Now listen up, and I'll tell you all where you're gonna be."

By late afternoon they were on the outskirts of Socorro.

"Now what?" Clint asked. "We can't just ride in there."

"No," Siringo said.

"Why not?" Horn asked. "If Sandusky is there, with his *segundo* and his woman, that's just what we gotta do."

"If they ran out of Juarez last night because of the shooting," Clint said, "then they know it was me."

"But do they know you were there lookin' for them?" Horn asked. "Do they even know there's a connection between us and you?"

"Maybe not," Clint said. "Maybe they're expecting me and Elfego Baca. Either way, they'll be ready."

"Or," Siringo said, "they ain't even here."

"What do you propose?" Clint asked him.

"I propose that I ride down there and see what's goin' on," Siringo said, "and you two stay here."

"Naw, I vote no on that one," Horn said.

"So do I," Clint agreed.

"What then?"

Clint stared at the town.

"Let's do it," he said.

"Do what?" Siringo asked.

"He means let's ride right in together," Horn said.

"What if it's an ambush?"

"You know what men like this are like," Clint said. "They'll get antsy and fire too soon. They'll be the ones who warn us."

"Besides," Horn said, "maybe it'll rattle 'em. Us ridin' in bold like that."

Siringo studied them both.

"Well, okay," he said, "if that's what you fellas wanna do."

"That's what we want to do," Clint said.

"Let's get it over with," Horn said.

Siringo shook his head and said, "I'd say you were crazy, except . . ."

"Except what?" Clint asked.

"Except I'm usually the one everybody thinks is crazy."

THIRTY-NINE

Anderson walked into the cantina. Sandusky was sitting at a table with a beer. Sitting across from him Delilah was nursing a beer of her own.

"The men are all in place, Harlan," Anderson said.

"Out of sight?"

"Oh, yeah."

"Bring the horses around to the back," Sandusky said. "If this goes wrong, we'll have to hit the trail again."

"Why don't we go out and fight?" Delilah asked. "I ain't afraid of the Gunsmith."

Sandusky stood up, took a step, and backhanded her across the face, knocking her to the floor.

"You sayin' I'm afraid of the Gunsmith?"

"N-No, Harlan."

"Then shut up," he said. "Don't open your mouth again unless I wanna put my cock in it."

"Yeah, sure, Harlan."

"Get up!"

She got to her feet and sat back down. Her big breasts

moved easily inside her shirt, which she had to readjust as she sat. Anderson watched.

"Cal!"

"Yeah?" Anderson said, still staring.

"Move those horses around the back."

"Yeah, sure, boss," Anderson said.

Anderson went out. Soon after they could hear the horses being moved.

"Delilah, you wanna go out there and shoot it out with the Gunsmith?" Sandusky asked. "Be my guest, honey." He sat down, wrapped his hand around his beer.

"No, Harlan," she said, "I'll stay in here with you."

Sandusky looked over at the Mexican barkeep, who stood quietly behind the bar.

"You got any whiskey?" he asked.

"Sí, señor."

"Bring me a bottle and a glass."

"Sí, señor."

But the man hesitated just a little too long.

"Wait a minute," Sandusky said. "Stand right there."

The man froze.

"Delilah, go see if there's a shotgun behind that bar."

"Sure, Harlan."

She got up and walked to the bar, a livid bruise showing on her cheek. Reaching over the bar, she came out with a twin-barrel Greener shotgun. She carried it to Sandusky and handed it to him.

"Twelve gauge," he said. "Nice gun." He looked at Delilah. "Siddown."

She sat.

"See these barrels? They ain't parallel. They fire so that the shot comes out and then intersects at a certain point, tears a man apart at a certain range. Further away the shot starts to spread, makes a whole different kinda mess."

He looked at the bartender.

"Bring me that whiskey!"

"Sí, señor."

The bartender grabbed a glass and bottle, carried them to Sandusky, and set them down on the table in front of him.

He uncorked the bottle, poured a shot, and drank it. Then he looked at Delilah.

"Want one?" he asked her.

"Sure, Harlan."

He poured another glass, shoved it across the table to her. She polished it off immediately.

Anderson came in, this time from the back.

"The horses are tied off behind this place, boss," he said.

"Good," Sandusky said. "Now we wait."

"What if they don't come?" Anderson asked.

"Then we'll just head back to the United States," Sandusky said. "Go on. Get out of here."

"I think I'd like it better that way," Anderson said.

"You're feelin' antsy, Cal?" Sandusky said. "Why don't you use that whore in the back?"

"No thanks," Anderson said. "I peeked in at her. She's fifty if she's a day."

"Well, take Delilah, then," Sandusky said.

"Harlan—" Delilah said.

"Go ahead," Sandusky said. "Take Delilah in the back, use 'er. Get some of those nerves out."

"Yeah, boss?"

"Yeah, sure," Sandusky said. "Go ahead. Anything happens, I'll let you know."

"Harlan—" she said again.

"Go on," Sandusky told her. "Show Cal a good time, Delilah."

"Sure, Harlan," she said. "Sure."

She stood up, walked to the back door, Anderson right behind her, a spring in his step.

FORTY

Clint, Siringo, and Horn rode into Socorro.

"They're here," Clint said.

"I can feel 'em," Horn said.

"You fellas are spooky," Siringo said.

"You spent too much time as a cowboy," Horn said. "Your nose is full of manure."

"Check the rooftops," Clint said.

It was dead quiet.

"Listen up real good," Horn said. "Somebody will cock their gun."

Siringo looked at Horn as if he was crazy, but he kept his ears open.

The instructions given to Kane and the men were, "Don't fire too soon. Don't make any noise. And don't anybody panic."

Well, that was easier said than done when dealing with someone like the Gunsmith.

The men were scattered on rooftops, and in deserted storefronts.

One scraped his foot on the wooden floor.

Another cocked the hammer on his gun.

A third coughed.

And then somebody panicked . . .

Clint, Horn, and Siringo heard the sounds just before the first hurried shot was fired. A bullet struck the dirt in front of them, and then they were off their horses as the snipers began to fire . . .

In the cantina Sandusky heard the shots. Anderson had been in the back for a while with Delilah, whose screams had died down. But he was sure they were still so busy they didn't hear the first shot. Maybe not even the ensuing shots. Sandusky knew from experience how much noise Delilah could make, even if she was just breathing hard in his ear. And he knew Anderson would be grunting like a pig.

He stood up and, taking the shotgun with him, went out the back door to the horses . . .

Horn jarred his injured leg as he hit the ground, but he quickly made his way to cover behind a dry horse trough. Normally the water made a trough good cover, but since this one was empty, there was a chance a bullet might go right through it. Still, he didn't have much choice . . .

Clint hit the ground with his gun already out. He held tight so it wouldn't be jarred from his hand. He spotted men with rifles on the rooftops, and fired. One man yelled, and fell off the roof. The air was soon filled with the sounds of shots . . .

* * *

Siringo thought to grab his rifle as he leaped from his saddle. He hit the ground hard, but came up onto one knee with the rifle pressed to his shoulder. He saw one man fall from the roof, fired, and took care of another one. He knew that the ambushers were firing wildly, but that he, Clint, and Horn would be firing calmly and accurately. Even outnumbered, this gave them an advantage.

Siringo got himself out of the street, took cover behind some crates.

There were shooters on both sides of the street. Clint and Siringo ended up taking cover on one side, and Horn on the other. Most of the shooters were on rooftops, but there were a few on the ground level, inside stores.

Clint saw a storefront with a broken front widow. There were two gun barrels sticking out.

"Cover me!" he shouted to Siringo.

He broke cover, ran over to that building, flattened his back against the wall. The overhang gave him cover from across the street, so he was virtually unseen by any of them.

He inched over to the window, and as a hand came out holding a gun, he grabbed it by the wrist and yanked. The man came tumbling out the window. Clint shot him before he could get his feet back under him.

The other man inside backed away from the window, but Clint stepped out, confronted him, and shot him.

Two more down . . .

Cal Anderson finally heard the sounds of the shots once he was done with Delilah. She lay on her back, big breasts flattened out against her chest, her legs wide open, black pubic bush covered with his semen. Her breasts were already starting to show bruises from where he'd gripped them cruelly.

"What the hell—" he said, getting to his feet.

Delilah rolled over and got her feet on the floor, reached for her clothes.

"Sounds like all hell has broke loose," he said, doing the same.

"We better get out there," she said dully.

"Too bad," he said, leering at her. "I was kinda hopin' to stick my dick in your ass."

"We're done, Cal," she told him, reaching for his gun.

"Yeah," he said, "unless Harlan says different."

"Harlan," she said, "can go to hell."

"I'd like to see you tell him that," he said, staggering as he tried to get his leg into his trousers.

"Maybe I will," she said, "but I'm gonna send you there first."

He was still hopping around on one leg when she shot him in the groin.

She was tired of being used . . .

FORTY-ONE

Horn shot two men on the roof across from him. One fell off, while the other staggered back. He didn't reappear, so Horn assumed he had killed him.

He studied the rooftops across from him, didn't see any more men. He saw Clint across the street, standing in front of a store where he had killed two men. Horn judged they had killed about six ambushers so far.

Not bad.

He started to ease himself from cover when suddenly a body fell from above him, almost landing on him . . .

Siringo fired at the roof, just above where Horn had taken cover. The man fell off the roof, and almost hit Horn, who had started to come out from behind the trough.

"Hey!" Horn yelled. "Watch it!"

"Sorry!" Siringo shouted.

Clint studied the rooftops in front of him, waiting for someone with a rifle to show himself. By his count they'd taken care of seven men.

He took himself back over to where Siringo was crouched.

"You see Sandusky?"

"No," Siringo said, "and I ain't seen a woman yet either."

Horn came walking across the street, reloading as he did.

"I heard some horses," he said. "I think the rest of them hightailed it."

Clint and Siringo also reloaded. All three kept their eyes peeled.

"Let's take a look around," Siringo said.

They walked down the street, aware that they were being watched from some windows, but apparently by denizens of Socorro, who had taken refuge from the firefight.

Finally, a door opened and a man crept out.

"Don't shoot, *señor*," he said, his hands up.

"Relax, old timer," Siringo said. "We're not gonna shoot you."

"They are all dead, *señores*," the man said. "You have killed them, or chased them off. *Gracias*."

"What about the leader, *señor*?" Clint said. "Where would he be?"

"They were using the cantina down the street," the old man said, pointing. "I am going to tell my people they may come out."

"Go ahead," Siringo said.

The three of them walked to the cantina and entered, guns in hand. The bartender stood behind the bar with his hands up.

"Where are they?" Siringo asked.

"They went out the back," the said. "They took my shotgun, *señores*."

"Thanks for the warning," Clint said.

They went through the back door, found it similar to the one in Juarez, rooms where whores could take their johns. They found a woman, too old to be a whore but obviously still working, in one of the rooms, and she waved her hands at them.

"No, no, no," she said.

"Take it easy, *señorita*," Clint said.

She calmed down when Siringo said something to her in Spanish. She replied at length.

"What'd she say?" Clint said.

"She says she's the only *puta* here, but that one of the men took a gringa woman into another room."

"Let's check it out," Clint said.

They moved farther down the hall, found a couple of empty rooms, then the room they wanted.

As they entered, the woman sitting on the bed looked up. She started to lift her gun, then decided against it and just let it drop from her hand. She looked like a once attractive woman who had lived a hard life. The room smelled like sex.

On the floor was a dead man, lying on his face, not even half into his trousers, a pool of blood around him.

"Is that Sandusky?" Clint asked.

Siringo bent over to look, but the woman spoke.

"No, that's Cal Anderson," she said. "Sandusky's second in command."

"And you?" Horn asked.

"Delilah," she said.

"Sandusky's woman?"

She nodded.

"Where is he?" the detective asked.

She shrugged, said, "He gave me to Cal, and while we

were in here, he left. Rode off. Our horses were in the back, but his is gone."

"Why did you kill him?" Horn asked.

She shrugged again. "Just tired of bein' used and bruised, I guess."

Horn left the room to check the horses and make sure she was telling the truth. He was back in seconds.

"She's right," he said. "One horse rode off."

"He used the commotion to get away," Clint said. "Probably hoped some or all of us would get killed."

"Are you Siringo?" she asked the detective.

"Yes."

"He talked about you," she said. Then she looked at Clint. "The Gunsmith?"

"That's right."

She looked at Horn. "You ain't Elfego Baca."

"No," he said, "Tom Horn."

"Baca had his own business to take care of," Clint said.

"So none of you is dead."

"No," Siringo said.

"Good," she said. "Then you'll catch him."

"Oh, we'll catch him," Siringo assured her. "Any idea where he went?"

"Yeah," she said. "He said he was going back to the U.S."

"We'll track him," Horn said. "We got 'em all except him."

"And you," Clint said to Delilah. "What should we do with you?"

"I don't really care," she said.

"Let her go," Siringo said.

"What?" Horn asked.

"He used 'er," Siringo said, "and tossed her away. What good does it do to put her in jail?"

"I agree," Clint said.

Horn shook his head. "You guys are soft."

The three of them looked at her one more time, then turned and left the room.

FORTY-TWO

Sandusky tried to shake them by switching horses frequently, riding in streams, doubling back, and eventually, riding from Texas into Louisiana.

It went on for weeks, and about the only good part was that Horn's leg was healing well.

"Is he heading for New Orleans?" Siringo wondered. "He'd stand out there."

"He's got to go through Baton Rouge first," Clint said. "Maybe we can catch him there."

"What about more men?" Siringo asked. "It seems to be his talent, picking up men to work with him."

"Unless the word gets around how he's been treatin' his men," Clint said, "givin' them up so he can get away."

"Well," Horn said, "judging from his tracks, he hasn't picked up anybody yet. But that doesn't mean he won't somewhere along the way."

"If I was him," Clint said, "somewhere in Louisiana I'd switch to the river."

"Hop on a riverboat upriver?" Siringo said. "That's a good idea, Clint. But maybe he ain't that smart."

"Or maybe he don't like boats," Horn said. "I know they make me sick."

"Well, whatever happens," Clint said, "we need to restock in Baton Rouge."

"We'll be there in an hour," Horn said. "And his tracks head straight there."

"When we get there, we might as well check on boats," Siringo said. "It's too good an idea to pass up."

"Agreed," Horn said.

Sandusky had decided he needed a boat.

Tom Horn was a tracker, a manhunter. As long as Horn was tracking him with Adams and Siringo and whoever else was with them, Sandusky needed to find a way not to leave a trail. That meant water.

He'd tried riding through streams, but that would only delay things. As he approached Baton Rouge, he realized he could catch a riverboat there and take it upstream to Vicksburg or Saint Louis.

Once he put the Mississippi between himself and them, they'd never catch him.

When they reached Baton Rouge, they decided before picking up any supplies that they'd better figure out whether Sandusky was there, had been there but had ridden on, or had gotten himself on a boat.

"I'll check the riverboats," Clint offered.

"I'll check the hotels," Horn said, because he didn't really want to go near the river.

"I'll talk to the local law, then see what I can find out

from the livery stables," Siringo said. "If all of that fails, we can check the saloons together."

They agreed, and split up.

Sandusky found a boat that would be leaving later that day. He had three hours to kill. One thing he wanted to do was sell his horse and saddle. He still had some money left over from the last job he'd pulled, but he didn't want to take the horse and saddle on the boat. He could buy new ones at the other end. He'd decided to take the riverboat—called *The Enterprise*—all the way up to Saint Louis.

He bought his ticket, and headed for the nearest livery stable to make a deal.

Clint checked with the harbormaster and found out that a boat would be leaving in the next hour or so.

"Is it here, or is it coming in?" he asked.

"It's here," he was told.

He went down to the river to take a look at *The Enterprise*.

Siringo tried three livery stables, and at the third one he heard that a man had recently sold his saddle and horse.

"Can I see them?"

"You wanna buy 'em?" the liveryman asked.

"No, I just wanna see them."

"Still gotta pay," the man said.

Siringo paid.

Horn was coming up empty, and was afraid he was going to have to go down to the harbor. His stomach was feeling queasy already.

* * *

Sandusky had his ticket and was just waiting for the call to board. He found a saloon near the harbor to wait in. He was told someone would come in and call for passengers.

Siringo found Clint on the river.

"I found his saddle and horse," he said. "He sold them to a livery close by."

"Are you sure they're his?"

"I checked the horse's hooves," Siringo said. "Horn said the animal he rode here had a cut on the left rear, and I found it."

"Well, I found one boat that's going out, and it leaves in about half an hour," Clint said. "We need to find him by then."

They saw Horn approaching them, a miserable look on his face.

"I didn't find anythin'," he said.

"We've pinpointed a boat we think he's takin'," Siringo said.

"We need to search these docks, and places nearby," Clint said. "Maybe he's in a saloon or a restaurant or café."

"One of us should stay by the boat, in case he tries to board," Siringo said.

"Tom, you're still limping, even though you're healing," Clint said. "Why don't you do that?"

Horn didn't want to be that close to the river, but he couldn't argue the point.

"Okay."

"Clint, you and me will split up and start searching. If he's alone, whoever finds him should just try to take him."

"Agreed," Clint said. "It's time to end this."

"We can't let him leave on that boat," Siringo said.

"I won't let him get on," Horn promised.

"And he's probably still got that shotgun he took from the bartender in Sirocco," Siringo said, "so be careful."

"Let's get it done," Clint said.

FORTY-THREE

A man stuck his head in the door and called for passengers for *The Enterprise*.

"Time to board!" he called out.

Sandusky grabbed his saddlebags and the shotgun and hurried out.

Siringo was checking cafés and saloons while Clint checked the docks. The detective walked past the saloon just as Sandusky came walking out.

They completely missed each other.

Sandusky headed for the boat, certain that he had made it. Still, he held the shotgun ready.

Clint spotted a man from behind, approaching the docks, and he studied him for a moment. He saw the saddlebags over his shoulder, and the shotgun in his hands, and decided this was his man.

* * *

Horn was scanning the faces of the people who were boarding. The area in front of *The Enterprise* had become
crowded. If he shot Sandusky, there'd be a lot of innocent
bystanders who might get hurt.

Sandusky had seen Tom Horn the day that Anderson shot
him. When he saw him by the gangway, he knew it was him.
He was still hidden from Horn's view by the other people.
    He stuck the shotgun out in front of him.

Clint lost Sandusky in the crowd, hurriedly tried to work
his way through to the boat. If Horn didn't see the man in
time . . .

Sandusky made sure he remained behind a group as they
approached the gangway. At the last moment he stepped out
and pointed the shotgun at Horn.
    "Time to die," he said.
    Horn went for his gun, but he wasn't as fast, and the shot-
gun was already pointed at him.
    He knew he'd never make it.

Clint saw Sandusky point the shotgun at Horn. The last thing
he wanted to do was shoot a man in the back, but he had no
choice. Even if he yelled, Sandusky might not hear him, or
might not turn.
    He drew and fired.

People screamed at the sound of the shot, and most of them
hit the ground. As the bullet struck Sandusky, he jerked the
shotgun up and it fired into the air.
    Horn stood with his hand on his gun.

* * *

Clint approached Sandusky with his gun still out, checked the body. He kicked the shotgun into the water, plucked the man's pistol out of his holster, and did the same with it.

"That was close," Horn said. "Thanks."

Siringo came running up with his gun out.

"It's over," Clint said.

"Clint saved my bacon."

People started standing up again, milling about, boarding the boat. A man came running down the gangway, looked like the captain of the boat. And soon, Clint figured, there'd be law.

"What's goin' on?" the captain demanded.

Clint ignored him and said to Siringo, "That's Sandusky, isn't it?" Horn took the captain aside.

Siringo turned the man over and said, "Yeah, that's him."

"So it's over," Clint said. "We'll just have to explain it to the law when they get here."

He ejected the spent shell, replaced it, and holstered his gun.

"You okay?" Siringo asked.

"I had to shoot him in the back."

"Oh," Siringo said. "You wouldn't have done it if you had another way."

"I know," Clint said, "but somehow, that doesn't make me feel much better."

"Well," Siringo said, putting his hand on Clint's shoulder, "you wouldn't be the man you are if it did."

Watch for

THE DEVIL'S COLLECTOR

379th novel in the exciting GUNSMITH series

from Jove

Coming in July!

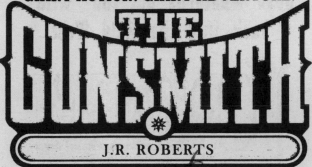

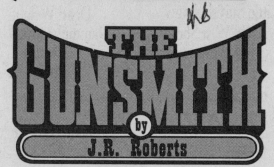
M11G0610